Hans J. Rokohl

Memories of West Berlin and West Germany

In the Shadow of the Wall, in the Light of the West

Bibliographic information of the German National Library: The German National Library lists this publication in the German National Bibliography; detailed bibliographic data is available on the Internet at dnb.dnb.de.

Automated analysis of the work in order to obtain information, in particular about patterns, trends and correlations in accordance with §44b UrhG ("Text and Data Mining") is prohibited.

Publisher: BoD · Books on Demand GmbH, Überseering 33, 22297 Hamburg, bod@bod.de

Printed by: Libri Plureos GmbH, Friedensallee 273, 22763 Hamburg

ISBN: 978-3-8192-6561-7

Table of Contents

Volume I

Stories from West Berlin and beyond

Preface to Volume I

To start with, all my stories are autobiographical and therefore true, albeit of a positive nature. Who wants to read about suffering and misery? There was, but only a little of it and I didn't dwell on it.

From the very beginning of my post-war memoirs, I not only talk about my experiences during this time, but also about the accompanying circumstances, which are commonly referred to as the events of the time. This continues into the years of the economic miracle.

In the Heimatgefühle aus Neu-Tempelhof I describe the world I lived in, with a bit of the city's history, and I haven't quite closed the chapter yet. Because Neu-Tempelhof is not only interesting from a historical point of view, but also in terms of urban development.

The 60s are about young love, nice trips and great cars, social interaction with friends and colleagues. There is also contemporary history. In the 70s, they say goodbye to grandma and look to the West, with lots of leisure time fun.

In the stories from Kurfürstendamm, I describe my experiences on this boulevard. It is also a journey through time, from the ruins of the memorial church to the boulevard in its festive splendor. From Bill Haley's rock and roll to Let it be by the Beates and Lets twist again. The song by Hildegard Knef is unforgettable.

My student Christmas stories form the conclusion. There are some curious things in there, but I don't want to give any more away.

I have illustrated the stories, most of them with my own photos, some of the pictures I have taken from the Internet, some from literature. I thought to myself, this way I can prove the stories in their reality.

The illustrated stories from West Berlin are followed in a second book by stories from West Germany, where I still spend the second half of my life.

Post-war memories

From the beginning

My post-war memories begin with the Allied air raids on the center of Berlin. Simeonstraße, where I lived with my mother and aunt, grandma and grandpa, was completely destroyed in the hail of bombs. Thus bombed out, the Beck family was assigned an apartment at Burgherrenstraße 11, not far from Tempelhof Airport. Grandpa was put to work repairing Me 109s and other fighter planes. I will tell you more about life in Burgherrenstraße in the post-war period, from the time of the economic miracle until I finished school. But what happened before that? How and in what circumstances did the Beck family live in Berlin-Mitte back then?

The idea came to me while reading a crime novel by Philipp Kerr. In the first book of his "Berlin Trilogy" (March Violets), he describes the impression his protagonist, private detective Berni Günther, got of Simeonstraße when he visited a Jewish fence there. Incidentally, the Kerr crime novels were the basis for Volker Kutscher's "Babylon Berlin".

From Alte Jakobstraße, which runs parallel to Lindenstraße, you can see Simeonstraße through the gate, followed by Wassertorstraße, where you can see the Evangelical Simeon Church. At the end you come to Prinzenstraße, where there was a crossing in GDR times. Kerr's protagonist describes Simeonstraße in 1936 something like this:

BERLIN. Alte Jakobstr. 3-4. Durchgang nach der Simeonstr.
436. Jm Hintergrund die St. Simeonskirche

"Simeonstraße was only a few streets away from Neuenburger Straße, but differed in that in Neuenburger Straße only the paint was peeling off the window frames, but in Simeonstraße the

window glass was missing. A really poor area. The 5- to 6-storey tenements stood high above the narrow cobbled street, over which clotheslines were stretched."

"Sullen youths loitered in the dark doorways, staring at the snot-nosed children playing noisily on the sidewalks, unimpressed by the swastika and hammer-and-sickle graffiti on the walls of the houses, not to mention the obscene images"

"Below the littered street level and in the shadows of the buildings were cellar stores offering goods and services. But there was no need for them."

The Beck family lived at Simeonstraße 7 for at least 20 years. This can be seen from daughter Ilse's birth certificate, which was issued by the Prussian Registry Office VI from 1924 to the end of 1944.

My mother and my aunt Ille spent their childhood there, went to elementary school and were baptized and confirmed in the Simeon Church. I was also baptized there. Grandma was very fond of this.

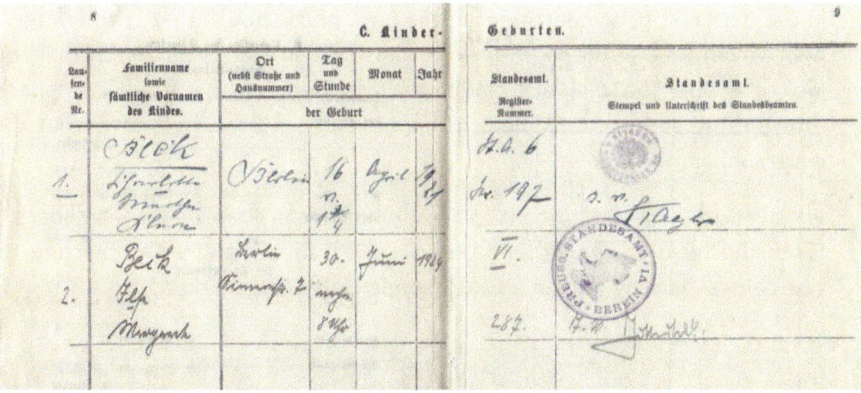

The picture shows the street around 1930. People are trading firewood for potato peelings. In the background you can see the passageway to Alte Jakobstraße, on the other side of the street, where passers-by are walking, you can see one of the cellar stores. The poor pavement can also be seen. If you were to walk in the other direction, you would reach Simeonkirche.

I

wonder if the Becks were queuing here too. And whether they lived all the time in the dark first floor apartment at the back of the house that I remember. In a photo from 1935 at the fountain in Urbanstraße in March, all four of them don't look like poor people, but rather well-dressed for the time. Perhaps Kerr exaggerated the circumstances in his novel. As a Scot, he knows that things were similar in Glasgow.

For the Becks, the assignment to Tempelhof was probably a gain, an apartment for the better-off. Even if they all lived in one room. Bright, with a balcony, there was central heating and an elevator, which later also worked.

Post-war memories

Simeonstrasse 1944/45

To anticipate, Simeonstraße no longer exists. It was completely destroyed during the war. You can still find it on previous city maps, see illustration.

We lived in this street at the time, in a rear building or side wing, on the first floor, the apartment was dark. Grandma and Grandpa probably had a janitor's job, and my mother and I and my Aunt Ilse (Ille) lived with them. I can't say why I lived there and not with my father as a family. My father had probably been there too. I know that from Grandma because I always had to put my left hand on the table when I ate.

At the end of 1944, Berlin-Mitte was completely destroyed by Allied air raids, because the backyard factories produced material that was vital to the war effort. The whole of Simeonstraße (see arrow) was also in ruins. Only the Simeon Church (see arrow), where I was baptized (see family book entry), remained standing.

There are photos of me and my mother from that year.

I can still remember one of those nights. Grandma or my mother dragged me across the burning ruins, my dark bobble hat over my head. We found accommodation with one of Grandpa's sisters, Frieda or Erna, in Jahnstraße in Kreuzberg. I still remember the wonderfully blue Mensch-Ärger-Dich-Nicht glass play figures.

After that we were evacuated from Berlin, my mother stayed with me and Grandma, Grandpa and Aunt Ille stayed in Berlin.

***

Leisten near Schnega 1945 to 1947

In Berlin, the bombing raids increased more and more. Mothers and their children were evacuated. My mother, grandmother and I came to Hitzacker on the Elbe, which is now part of the Lüchow-Dannenberg district in Lower Saxony. The area became famous for anti-nuclear demonstrations against the final repository for radioactive waste that was to be built there. There is still a photo of me sitting there looking after the allied air units on their flight to Berlin. Maybe I'll find it.

Then we were assigned to the Müllers in Leisten near Schnega, see map below. The Müllers had a farm in the Lower Saxon style, as shown here. The house consisted of a residential part and a barn part. In the barn there was a gallery with rooms for maids and farmhands. Now we were quartered there. Downstairs were the cattle, some cows and two horses in the stables, upstairs on the gallery were the chicken nests. There were also lots of fleas.

My mother and grandma made themselves useful in the household, after all, the pigs had to be fed too. I, on the other hand, was less useful. When the farmer's wife asked me if I had stolen another egg, I sheepishly said yes. My mother's head turned red every time. Well, sugar eggs were my favorite food. I wasn't a good little boy in other ways either. Once I was gone, half the village was looking for me. I think I had gone to a soccer match in Schnega. I don't know whether I was picked up there or, more likely, whether I was standing outside the door again. But I still remember the wooden pattens on my bottom.

Grandpa, meanwhile, who worked as a saddler repairing airplane seats in the hangars at Tempelhof Airport, was given an apartment nearby at Burgherrenstraße 11. That meant a room in a four-room apartment on the fourth floor, which he had to share with Aunt Ille. Another room was occupied by Mrs. Kater and son Charles. In mid-June 1946, Aunt Ille, now married, moved in with her husband's family. My cousin Wolfgang was born in October. We stayed in Leisten with the Müllers because the supply situation in Berlin was catastrophic. Also because my mother had her appendix taken out in the next town, I think it was Uelzen. She almost died from it. She was left with a large, disfiguring scar. In the summer of 1947 I was of school age, but not fit for school. I had to leave my sugar-egg paradise, but I didn't have to listen to the squealing of the stabbed pigs any more.

Here you can see the line from Berlin to Schnega today. The hamster trains certainly ran like this back then.

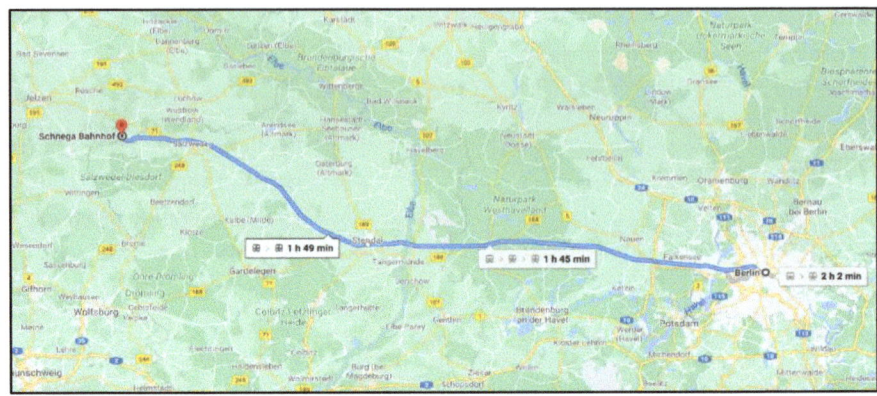

Burgherrenstraße 11 - 1947 to 1949

On the map you can see where Burgherrenstraße house no. 11 is located, see arrow. Me and the neighborhood children, and those from Dudenstraße 11

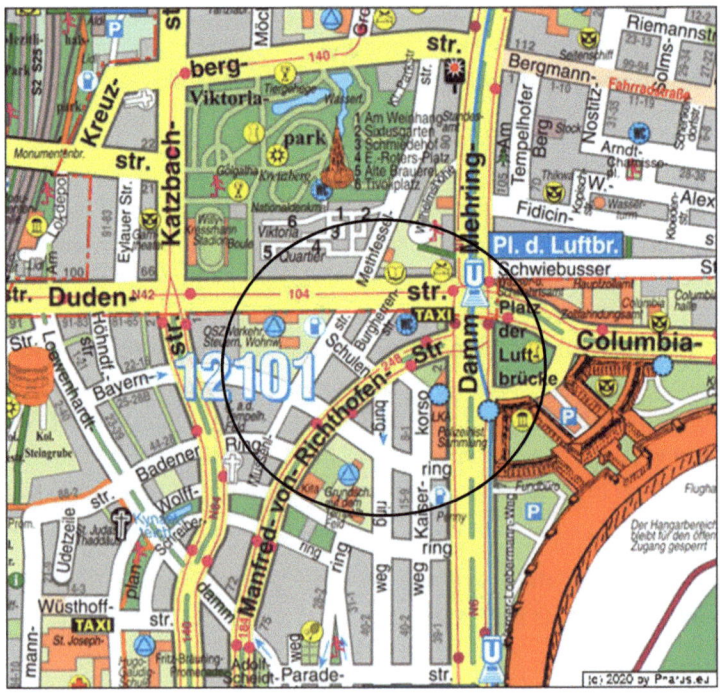

around the corner, played in the street. Small Karee: Burgherrenstraße, Schulenburgring, Methfesselstraße, Dudenstraße. Large Karee: Dudenstaße, Platz der Luftbrücke, Manfred-von-Richthofen-Straße, Schulenburgring. Otherwise in the Kaiser-Corso, in winter with the sledges up the Kreuzberg (Viktoriapark).

So my mother, grandma and I were back in Berlin, now in Tempelhof. How the four of us lived in one room is a mystery to me. Thank goodness Aunt Ille was staying with her husband's family. I once visited her secretly, Grazer Damm so and so at Kiefer. She stood there in the kitchen like Cinderella in a fairy tale and couldn't shut her mouth. I was only a good seven years old. She then brought me back. Soon afterwards, my marriage to Hans Kiefer ended in divorce, he got custody of my son Wolfgang and Aunt Ille had to move out. There were five of us in Burgherrenstraße.

I don't remember the currency reform, the subsequent blockade and the founding of the Federal Republic of Germany, but rather the conditions associated with it. You could buy something with the new money if you had more than the allotted 60 + 20 DM, I got something from the school meals and the others got social food. Grandpa kept rabbits on the balcony to eat. I can still see the skinned animals in front of me. The best thing was going to the Grunewald forest with Grandpa to collect firewood. The district heating in the apartment didn't work back then.

I have already written elsewhere about the school drama at the then 6th Tempelhof elementary school, now the Tempelherren School. Here I have recorded the route to school that my friend Volker Seidlitzski and I took for years. The buildings of the above-mentioned Karees were still intact, behind them in the direction of the church there was only rubble piled up on the street

I have already written elsewhere about the school drama at the then 6th Tempelhof elementary school, now the Tempelherren School. Here I have recorded the route to school that my friend Volker S. and I took for years. The buildings of the above-mentioned Karees were still intact, behind them in the direction of the church there was only rubble piled up on the street.

Post-war memories

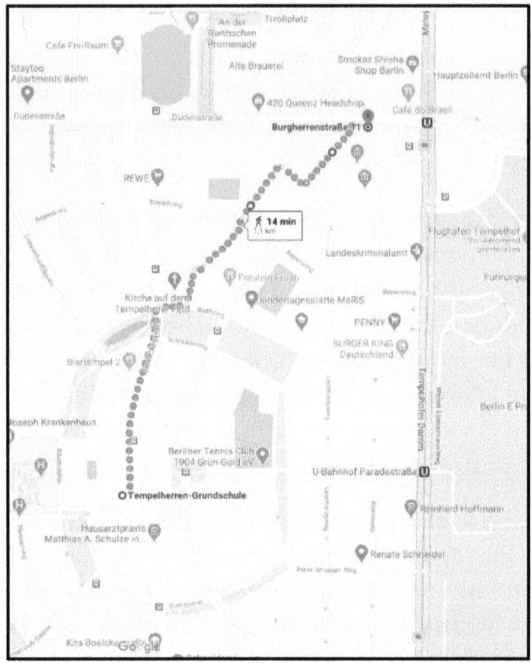

Here is another photo of me, taken on 27.07.1947, shortly before I started school. The white sweater is knitted from sugar sack yarn. You can see the discomfort on my face. A hard time for children too.

Post-war memories

Burgherrenstraße 11 - 1949 to 1953

After the founding of the FRG, Berlin retained its four-power status. Along the border to the Soviet sector, white signs with the inscription "You are leaving the American sector..." were posted everywhere.

At Burgherrenstraße 11, everyone tried to keep their heads above water. Aunt Ille worked as an assistant in a print shop. She later found a job somewhere near Frankfurt am Main (Taunus), away from the cramped living conditions in Berlin. She traveled a lot, probably invited. There is a photo of her posing in front of a convertible. My mother met her future husband in 1948, but they didn't get married until 1952. I remember that "Uncle Kurt" first lived in a furnished apartment in Kleineweg, but then went to work in France in between. My mother received a widow's pension and I received a half-orphan's pension. In return, I had to go to the police station in Neu-Tempelhof at regular intervals, it was terrible, like being paraded. At the beginning of the 1950s, my mother and Kurt moved together to Eisenacher Straße in Schöneberg. I stayed with Grandma and Grandpa, probably less because of the cramped living conditions there and more because Grandma thought I would be better off in Burgherrenstraße. Grandpa found work in the emergency program, see picture.

Elementary school was terrible for the first few years, then it got better. I kept up with the lessons. Volker S. and I took it in turns to be the final lanterns. We should have had extra lessons and remedial teaching, but no one thought of it. We were also lazy and just wanted to play. The two photos show a happy bunch of boys. That was a carefree time

Like a good half of the class, I then went on to secondary school, which at the time was called the secondary school of the practical branch (9th OPZ). There was also the technical branch for those who did well in English and the scientific branch for the really good students. We had two high-flyers who went to the

Post-war memories

Askanier-Gymnasium from year 5 onwards branch for the really good students. We had two high-flyers who went to the Askanier-Gymnasium from year 5 onwards.

Burgherrenstraße 11 - 1953 to 1956

In mid-summer 1953, Walter M. suddenly appeared at the door of Burgherrenstraße 11 after eight years as a Russian prisoner of war. I didn't know Uncle Walter, but Grandma and Grandpa did. He had become engaged to my Aunt Ille during the war or shortly before. There's a photo of the two of them, he in uniform, she still a girl. You can clearly see the engagement rings on their left ring fingers. So, the two moved in together, first to a room in Tiergarten and then, probably already married, to an apartment in Haselhorst. A year later, they had a daughter.

My mother and my stepfather Kurt found a new-build apartment in a social housing project in Schöneberg, Geßlerstraße. 4th floor, 2 rooms plus balcony, central heating. What more could you want? But - from then on they were called Merten. Now only grandma and grandpa and I lived at Burgherrenstraße 11. I got the little girls' room. Here is the floor plan of the apartment with the respective occupancy.

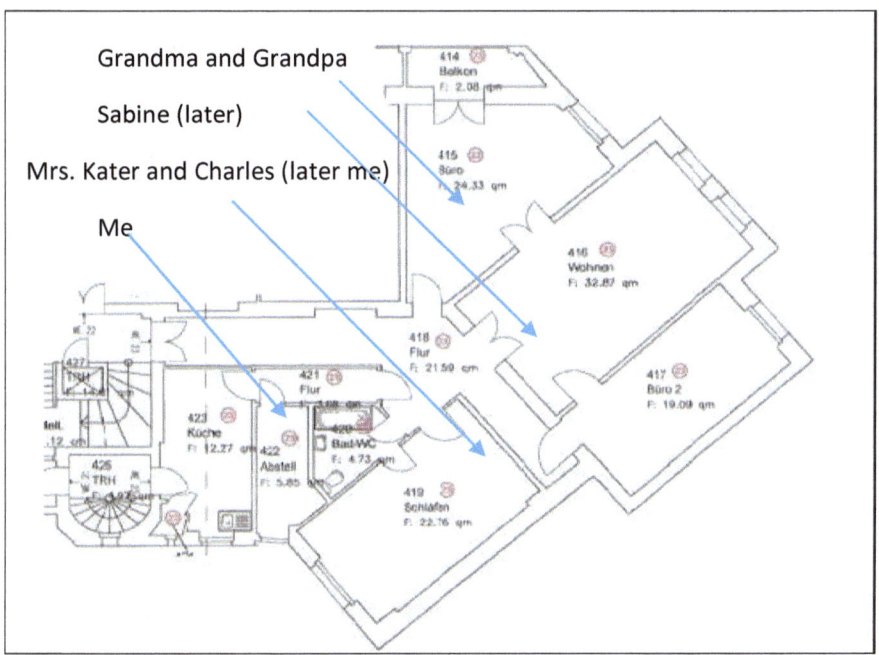

Grandma and Grandpa

Sabine (later)

Mrs. Kater and Charles (later me)

Me

Television in the new apartment

Things slowly started to look up. Everyone had work: Grandpa worked again as a fine bag maker well past his retirement age. Didn't stop until he was 75. My uncle Kurt worked as a "staircase terrier" (conductor) for the BVG, my mother as a cleaner. Uncle Walter became an authorized signatory for a large painting company.

Grandma and Aunt Ille were housewives. I did quite well at secondary school. The building trade advertised "Be smart, go into construction". I started an apprenticeship as a carpenter at Stöve Zimmerei. The Merten couple bought a

Post-war memories

VW Beetle. As the slogan on the right says, *"Full throttle into the economic miracle".*

Burgherrenstraße 11, 4th floor, right - What has remained

What has remained? From the outside, a West Berlin apartment with a post-war history, as in many other households in Berlin; from the inside, a shared home, almost a community of destiny.

Grandpa lived there until his death in 1979. Almost 35 years, 30 of them together with Grandma. I lived there, although not all the time. In the end, I had the Frau-Kater room as my Berlin visiting room. Grandpa was happy when I didn't come alone. What remains are the memories of my school days, the time of my training and further education and my student years.

I was a real grandma's child. No desire to go to school - lots of excuse slips. Something sweet with cola for breakfast, my teeth were getting worse and worse. But playing with Mrs. Kater's son Charly and my friend Volker was great. Others wondered what would become of the child.

My mother and Uncle Kurt came to the birthdays and holidays, as did Aunt Ille with Uncle Walter and later with my cousin Christiane. It was always a happy celebration. Gifts were always handed out. The big room was rented to Sabine, a young woman who worked as a trainee at a newspaper, I think it was the Tagesspiegel. She had met a nice American, with whom she later moved to California. Greetings from over there came from time to time. Grandpa usually argued with Mrs. Kater about the gas bill. After every cooking session, the meter had to be read and the consumption allocated to the respective household. We had a few visits from the American military police. Mrs. Kater had taken up with a Mr. Johnson, who served at Tempelhof Airport, but was probably better off with Mrs. Kater.

I'll spare you any more stories. The more interesting question is whether I would want to live there again. Because the apartments there are for sale. See the corresponding exposé below. Such an apartment would be nice, but no longer suitable. Let's leave it at the memories, the nice ones and the not so nice ones.

Post-war memories

3rd floor: 4 1/2 room old building apartment with balcony and elevator near Bergmannkiez in Tempelhof

Burgherrenstraße 11,12101 Berlin-Tempelhof, Berlin

Purchase price 730,000 €

Living space approx. 150 m²

Property description

This stately residential and commercial building on the corner of Burgherrenstrasse and Dudenstrasse was built in 1913. The entrance is particularly impressive: Beautiful natural stone strips on the walls and stucco elements on the ceiling emphasize the stately impression. The belt cornices have been preserved from the original stucco decorations. The residential building consists of a front building adjoining a small courtyard and a side wing with its own inner courtyard. The commercial premises are located on the first

floor of the front building, with apartments on all other floors and in the side wing. In total, Burgherrenstrasse 11 has six commercial units and 21 stately apartments of various sizes. Many of them have a large balcony or a beautiful bay window.

***

Feelings of home from Neu-Tempelhof

A foreword

I have allowed myself to be inspired. From two revered poets and storytellers: Wilhelm Raabe and Theodor Fontane. I came to Raabe when senior teacher Rockstroh taught us German literature philologically, not just tried to. I wrote a quote from Goethe for my A-levels, which we had never studied. Raabe wrote his "Chronik der Sperlingsgasse" as a young man from the perspective of an old man. That is certainly more difficult than trying to do it the other way round, as I intend to do.

Fontane, like Raabe, a representative of poetic realism, focused more on the places with his "Wanderungen durch die Mark". In his novels, for example in "Stechlin", he tells wonderful stories about his protagonist. These are not big stories, but rather small incidents with a time reference.

So much for the literary background. Now to the place, or rather a district in Berlin, just as manageable as the Spree Island in Berlin, where Sperlingsgasse is located, or Fontane's Neuruppin. Neu-Tempelhof was created just over a hundred years ago. It was created as an urban development project. But a lot has happened there.

Where did the name come from? - A memory

The memory first. The pond of the old Tempelhof village church was frozen over. As schoolboys, we had to try out whether the ice would hold. It didn't for me, so I collapsed, standing in ice-cold water up to my chest. But it happened so close to the embankment that I was able to crawl out. It got really cold on the way home. Because Alt-Tempelhof is not Neu-Tempelhof, at the northern end of which was Burgherrenstraße, where I used to live. The wet clothes on the line and me under the warm shower, or was it a warming bath after all.

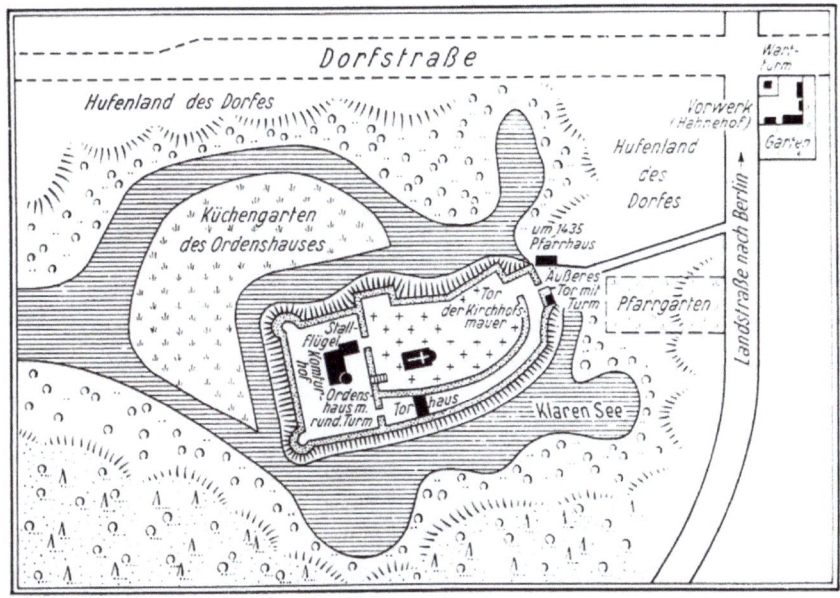

Such an event gives me reason to write about the naming of my home district. The additions ...Tempelhof and Burgherren... The church stands out for its defensiveness, firmly built from fieldstone. It was part of the Commandery of St. George of the German Knights Templar. The castle courtyard looks like this from a model from 1878: The church centrally located, with a wall surrounded by a lake. The country road to Berlin is now called Tempelhofer Damm and the village road is now called Alt-Tempelhof, even though it is now located further north. The place where I drew the cross is the site of my little accident.

So these were the Knights Templar on the Teltow plateau with their castle, who gave their name to the Tempelhof district and the street where I lived. The white coat with the red cross can be found on the coat of arms of Berlin-Tempelhof. The land belonged to the Sovereign Order of the Knights Templar and extended to the gates of the then twin city of Berlin-Cölln. At the beginning of the 20th century it was called Neu-Tempelhof.

The Master of the Order said: "In the name of the Father and the Son and the Holy Spirit, I make you a Knight of the Ordo Militiae Crucis Templi. Be you, my brother Lambertus, a brave, faithful, just and faithful knight of our Lord Jesus Christ and his Holy Temple. Stand up, my brother Lambertus, and receive the cross and mantle of the Order." This is not a scene from the Middle Ages: on Saturday evening in June 2012, the postulant received his knighthood at the altar of the 800-year-old village church.

A birthplace and more

Home and birthplace are inextricably linked. At the time of my birth, the "Third

Reich" was at war with the rest of the world, and shortly before that Hitler had the Soviet Union invaded. I was born in St. Josef's Hospital in Neu-Tempelhof. It was quite dramatic, my grandmother still had to donate blood to the young mother. Less than a year later, I was already grown up. I was still living with my grandparents in Berlin-Mitte. Pastor Boehm baptized me there in the Simeon Church on 26 October 1941. But I am a real Tempelhofer, my birth certificate was issued at the Berlin-Tempelhof registry office. I became a new Tempelhofer at the end of the war, when Allied bomber units bombed the center of Berlin. As a bombed-out person, my grandfather was assigned rooms in Neu-Tempelhof, not far from Tempelhof Central Airport. When I started school, I also lived at Burgherrenstraße 11. Gone were the good times on the Wendish farm where we evacuees lived.

About my birthplace: St. Joseph Hospital was one of the first Catholic hospitals in Berlin, opened earlier than planned in December 1928 due to an influenza epidemic. There was no hospital in the Tempelhof district until then.

The financing was unusual: Berlin Provincial Superior Sister M. Ewalda Weinrich published an appeal in several Berlin newspapers for the subscription of bonds. By the end of 1926, 1 million Reichsmark had already been collected. This

Feelings of home from Neu-Tempelhof

money formed the basis for the purchase of a 30-hectare plot of land in Neu-Tempelhof and the construction of the hospital. The St. Joseph Hospital was built in 18 months, a hospital of short distances with 600 beds, at a total cost of 6 million Reichsmark.

The war left its mark: partial destruction from bombing raids. In 1945, a German fighter plane crashed into the hospital, killing four people.

For 30 years, the church integrated into the hospital was also a place of worship for the Catholic parish of Neu-Tempelhof. And then in 1983 it became an academic teaching hospital for the Free University of Berlin.

I became acquainted with St. Joseph Hospital once again. As a young boy, I had to overcome gastritis. It was caused by poor dental health. I can still remember the resolute head nurse in the white habit of the Elisabeth nurse. And also the "sermon" of the young dentist. Both were enough to do something about it and

not rely on the inscription above the main portal: "Deus Provedebit" God will provide.

Feelings of home from Neu-Tempelhof

With the 98 through the Fliegerviertel

Until it was discontinued in 1961, the 98 streetcar was the only means of public transport on rails that ran right through Neu-Tempelhof. All the others ran around it, so to speak: the subway line 6 along or under Tempelhofer Damm to the side of the airport, the S-Bahn on the main line parallel to the border with Schöneberg, the 19 bus along Dudenstraße, which marked the border with the Kreuzberg district, and the S-Bahn on Berlin's Südring to Alt-Tempelhof.

If we wanted to visit our relatives in Lichterfelde, we took the 98 at the corner of Mehringdamm / Platz der Luftbrücke. The square in front of Tempelhof Airport was renamed after the Berlin Blockade. The streetcar then turned into Manfred-von-Richthofen-Straße, the largest street in the Fliegerviertel. The next stop was at Adolf-Scheidt-Platz, centrally located in Neu-Tempelhof, with a beautiful stork fountain. Unfortunately, there was also the police station, where I had to present myself and my mother at regular intervals in order to receive my half-orphan's pension. I always felt like I was being put on the spot.

I continued on the 98 via Werner-Voss-Damm to Boelckestraße, then through the S-Bahn tunnel to Manteuffelstraße, then westwards and for a very long time to Lichterfelde.

In the 60´s

Who wants to see hard-working craftsmen

The only craftsmen in the group photo are Heinz B. (1st from right) and Chairman of the Works Council, Otto Sch. (3rd from left) and Deputy Chairman of the Works Council and Treasurer. Semi-skilled welders are the 2nd from left

(I don't know his name) and the 2nd from right ("Piotr"). The one on the far left is Paul R., cal factor of the company and Heinz's father-in-law. The one almost in the middle is me, I don't know if I was still an apprentice sheet metal worker, but I'd already passed my skilled worker exam and the company took me on. Good skilled workers were in short supply back then. The photo was taken in the early sixties of the last century J. Hansen Stahlmöbelbau was a typical Berlin backyard business in Waldemarstraße (Berlin SO 36). The front building with driveway was a residential building. The junior boss, a dreaded creep by the way, and one of the two foremen lived there. The side wing housed the warehouse, the cutting room and, above that, the foreman's workshop and offices. In the five-storey rear building were the workshops (paint shop and assembly, medical cabinet construction, tubular furniture construction/upholstery), all connected by an industrial elevator.

Our department produced the well-known swinging chairs under license, swivel chairs, recliners and women's chairs as well as custom-made products. As you can see, I am currently straightening a swivel chair frame on the straightening plate. Back then, the frames still had (unsafe) four legs. Apart from that, I bent the cantilever chairs on the bending machine, cut pipes and built drawers for the sheet metal cupboards. I also made sure we had enough beer (Schuldheiß beer, various types) when Paul was ill or on vacation. I built a single-door medicine cabinet for testing. It wasn't quite angular, but it was enough and it sold well. Theoretically, I was in a good mood.

As you can easily imagine, Heinz and Otto made me a member of the IG Metall trade union and made me a union shop steward. I was allowed to go to training (in Lohr am Main, my first flight) and had to hold a works council election, nah yes. After I left, I often spent time with my colleagues Heinz and Otto in private. And the best thing was to annoy the junior boss by openly driving to work in the MGA roadster with Heinz on board. Heinz always said, "What a completely new driving experience!"

The car freaks of Tempelhof

What did people do in the early sixties when they had finished school and were able to live cheaply and comfortably in Hotel Mama or Grandpa? Buying a trendy sled was the first choice. A new car was out of the question, as was a used one on installments.

The car needs of the protagonists pictured were different. My friend Peter K. was no longer allowed to drive his father's Borgward Aralla because of dents and needed a larger car, if only to extend his living space for visiting ladies. So it was an Opel Rekord, two-tone with a manual gearbox.

I already had a steep career behind me as far as cars were concerned, as I was 2 years older than Peter. The MGA Roadster shown here, light blue, with side windows and a hardtop for the winter, was my third car. After my apprenticeship, it was a VW Beetle Standard, still paid for in cash, could be driven with intermediate throttle, cable brakes, but no pretzel rear window and folding side indicators. It was too pop for me, something representative was needed and the well-known car dealership Ricci & Wichmann (in Wilmersdorf) had a beautiful Karmann Ghia, whitewall tires, pearl white. It didn't just run on gasoline, but on alternates. If one of them burst, the remaining debt became due immediately or the car was sold. Then the Karmann with its VW Beetle engine was no longer fast enough. So he went to Ricci & Wichmann to buy an English sports car.

The pictures were taken in a parking lot at Columbiadann. The two young gentlemen stand possessively on their respective treasures. Peter's car is not yet completely free of the bubonic plague. The right fender had been damaged. The Marchal headlights on the MG (Morris Garage) catch the eye. These expensive things (200 DM each) simply had to go.

Even today, after 50 years, they are still friends. And, as you can imagine, these were by no means the last cars. Peter recently had four (a 3-series convertible, a Bitter vintage car, a Mercedes 500 and an Opel Monza, and he sold another Bitter (which was an independent design based on the Opel Diplomat) for good

money. I adapted myself to the respective circumstances: After the MG (my fiancée's tousled hair always flew away), the big Karman Ghia, then a Diane during my time at Berlin College (was the better duck), a silver Beetle at university, then one of those first "junk" Golfs (with automatic) and to this day the BMW 1, 3 and 5 Series models.

In the 60´s

We weren't the only ones infected by the car virus back then. Our whole friendship indulged in this consumer idiocy. One of us always drove the bigger car. And off we went to Villa Marina de Cesenatico, to Julius and to repair and inspect the various Alfa Romeos.

We remained freaks, but in different ways. Today, Berlin's traffic conditions make it difficult for the enthusiasts. There is always a traffic jam on Tempelhofer Damm. Driving out and parking is no longer possible. But Peter doesn't use the BVG. I'm glad that I almost live in the country.

Fashion from Lichterfelde

Who are the three in the snow, or rather the three on the benches? When and where was the photo taken? It must have been in the early 60s and the place is Marienplatz in Lichterfelde. Right where the young lady with the fur collar lived. The collar and coat belonged to Roswitha J., the young man had decided not to wear a coat in view of his female companion. The young woman with the winter jacket was called Gerlinde.

Things were already fashionable back then, considering that all the people pictured were barely over twenty. I can no longer say whether Roswitha sewed her coat herself as a dressmaker, it was probably bought, as chic as it is. A suit with a dark tie and white shirt was compulsory back then, even outside in the March snow. Gerlinde was wearing a jacket similar to a poncho, with some kind of ski pants, tight but without stretch.

The

young couple actually fit together quite well. She is leaning elegantly against the birch tree, her hair up, looking at her partner, he is more casual, looking back. All that's missing is a hug and a snog.

What is there to say about the two young ladies? I was friends with Roswitha for quite a long time. I met her in a youth club in Steglitz. She lived in Grandpa's villa in Bassermannweg with her parents and two sisters, Renate and Gisela. Her father was a lawyer, her mother was very nice. It could have been something with the two of us. My dear friends Peter and Renate K. were very close to her until her death. She was married, and after the separation she bought a nice condominium on Kleiner Wannsee from her inheritance. She had a lingerie store nearby. The store ran like clockwork.

I can't say much about Gerlinde. We had arranged to go ice skating once. That was about it. All I heard from Peter was that she stayed unmarried and wasn't

doing well. If you look at the two of them in the picture, they seem to be pretty close. Yes - they were still doing well back then.

***

In the 60´s

May Day 1965 in front of the Reichstag

It was still very fresh on this May Day. The trees in the Tiergarten were not yet green, but the colorful ribbons were fluttering on the large maypole. The square in front of the Reichstag was already full of people. Even the little ones had to come along in baby carriages. Suits and ties were the order of the day.

That was the time of the big May Day rallies; up to six hundred thousand people usually came, a quarter of West Berlin's population. "Responsibility for Berlin - Responsibility for Germany" was the big slogan on the Portikus. Not the Federal Republic (...). Three years had passed since the Wall was built and when you walked around the Reichstag building, you suddenly stood in front of it. On the East Berlin side, everything was easy to hear, but the West side had made sure of that.

That's how close you got to prominent people at that time, here the Governing Mayor Willy Brandt. The couple to the right of the center could be Egon Bahr and his wife. Two years later, Willy was Chancellor and Egon (not Mielke) was State Secretary and then Minister. But we didn't know that yet.

Five years later, everything was different. The '68ers were walking through Wedding, and even later through Kreuzberg, "celebrating" Labor Day in their own way - until the police intervened (in hundreds). The East German treaties negotiated by Brandt and Bahr were forgotten. Today, the Chancellor looks out onto Platz der Republik, sees the tourists in the dome of the building, not a trace of trade unionists.

Off to the lido with the girls

As children and teenagers, we often went to the Strandbad Wannsee. We walked to Tempelhof S-Bahn station, changed to the Wannseebahn at Schöneberg station and got off at Nikolassee, one station before Wannsee, i.e. where the piers are. All for 30 pfennigs. You then had to walk a bit over the "Spinnerbrücke" bridge to the entrance. And then you stood there and had a wonderful view of the Wannsee.

Incidentally, *the spinners* were motorcyclists who rode down from the bridge on the AVUS towards the Funkturm (radio tower). The motorcycle from back then (early 1950s) was a Horex Regina 400 ccm. You can't get it for less than €8,000 on eBay today. More on this at the end.

After the war, for large sections of the West Berlin population, the Wannsee lido was a substitute for a trip to the seaside, which very few people could afford in the early post-war years. It felt a bit like being at the seaside. There were sun loungers and beach chairs to rent, changing rooms and those who didn't want to lie in the sand could make themselves comfortable on the terraces.

In the 60´s

In the years when these photos were taken (mid-60s), I went there with the girls in my car and we only stayed for a few hours, not the whole day. I knew Sigrid, the one with the white headscarf, from childhood, she was a neighbor from

Dudenstraße 11 (just around the corner). She had trained as a shoe saleswoman and worked in a fancy shoe store on Kurfürstendamm. We were already friends, but not in a relationship. The other young woman was probably a colleague. I think the girls just wanted to be taken out by a nice young man. And why not?

Now to another beauty: Regina. I think she had a royal wave. That's not a hairstyle, it was used to control the valves of an engine. But it only looked like one, it was

just a protective tube for the two tappets on the hanging valves. Kingshafts are still around today, on the Ducati 750 and Kawasaki W800. Back then, our beauty had 22 hp and made a smooth 130 km/h. It was really fast.

A romantic trip to the south

Newly engaged and off to the south, taking their annual vacation. After all, the fiancées were in paid employment, she as a mid-level civil servant in the telecommunications office (that was Telecom at the time) and he as a metalworker in a medium-sized company. So, at least three weeks paid vacation.

A trip to the south is chic and fine for others, sung by the young Cornelia Fröbes in 1962, was taken literally by the two of them, because they were the others. Unlike in the song, in which Tina and Marina wanted to take the D-train to Naples, Hans and Monika preferred to travel by car. It's too far from Berlin to Naples, so Lake Garda would do. With a legitimate claim to a double room, the engaged couple moved into a pretty hotel in Malcesine on Lake Garda.

Let's move on to "chic and fine". That was the time of "Double Income - No Kids". In the case of the fiancées, hotel mom or grandma and not giving up any of the money they earned. Starting a family tended to happen unexpectedly. If they did, then traveling was no longer an option. So the combination of a fancy car and trips abroad was something to strive for. This was also the case for the engaged couple.

In the 60´s

The travel car was an MGA roadster, light blue, 90 hp. Really something to show off, just not a touring car. There was just enough room for a suitcase behind the two seats, but nothing more, because the spare wheel was in the trunk. Of the unpleasant features in the appropriate place every now and then.

Even on the outward journey, the car became increasingly difficult to steer, which was remedied by lubricating the steering linkage. As a result, we arrived late at the hotel, happy that nothing else had happened. Here is the view from the hotel parking lot. As you can see, 600cc Fiats parked on the road.

There were some nice views down to the lake, like here on the lakeside promenade.

An attempt was made to steal the sports car at night, but this was unsuccessful due to the complicated starting mechanism. There were no further attempts.

These are now pictures of newlyweds. You can see how much happiness and love goes into eating a melon.

And driving around Lake Garda was really fun in a spot car. The Gardesana Orientale leads around Lake Garda,

with differences in altitude, steep slopes, galleries and tunnels. Something hip in an open car.

The two fiancées are just 22 and 24 respectively, as you can see from the posing shots. Would that be possible nowadays, when many people at this age are studying for a bachelor's or perhaps even a master's degree? Isn't romantic travel possible without higher education? The two still seemed unconcerned.

The highlight of the trip was Venice. The Grand Canal was calling, St. Mark's Square, the Doge's Palace, the Bridge of Sighs and so on. Piazzale Roma was full. For a good tip, the car could be parked in an underground garage. As my fiancé at the time, I was there again, now married for many years, recently returning

from a cruise. No more parking spaces, just a huge bus station. Otherwise, the lagoon town has hardly changed, as the pictures show.

It's about 180 km from Malcesine to Venice, a good two and a half hours by car, but not in this sports car. The long-stroke engine (four-cylinder in-line engine) had to cool down every hour in the heat outside. It was designed for English weather and country roads, and not for the Autostrada del Venezia. The return journey from Venice was no better.

On our farewell evening, the two fiancées went out for a fancy dinner. A great restaurant with a terrace overlooking the lake. And above all, they drove up and posed in style.

Getting back to Berlin was also a pain. Not only because of the distance of 975 km, but also because of the blocked first gear. It didn't look good at the border controls to start in second gear. Eventually it was done. Less than a year later, the car was replaced by a nice German model.

Was it really a romantic vacation with a car like that? It seemed to be, according to the motto: We can master even greater things (in love).

Ascension Day 1967 - Father's Day without fathers - on land and on water

Father's Day in Berlin is actually celebrated in a Kremser, a spacious covered wagon with longitudinal benches, invented by a horse-drawn bus entrepreneur of the same name, with a carriage ride through the Grunewald forest. Until everyone is full. The three of us, now state-certified graduates of the evening school for technicians at the Beuth Engineering Academy (we couldn't go any longer), turned it into a short boat trip on the Unterhavel. This will now be shown and explained in pictures.

In the 60´s

Around the middle of the Havelchaussee we unpacked: my Inka S inflatable boat (red), the Johnson outboard motor with 3 hp, the crate of Berlin beer. Everything from my 1600 Karmann Ghia (white, black trim, 50 hp), trunk in the front. Friedel has to fortify himself with the first

Stubbi (according to DIN 6199) while pumping up. The clothes are correct, the road is still empty and the trees are green and in bloom. I am in charge of supervision.

Now the boat is inflated and the engine transom is in place, all that's missing is the floor inlet. Now I lend a hand too.

Notice my smart sailing sweater, trimmed in white, and white boat shoes. Friedel has lit a little pipe, in the style of the time.

Everyone lends a hand, that's not true, someone has to hold the line.

As you can see, white shirts and ties are the order of the day. This is clothing for yacht owners who handle the dinghy. Or just the appropriate one for Father's Day.

So now I've reached the shore. I also lend a hand. Next door is the landing stage of the Stern-und-Kreis-Schifffahrt. It must have been quite chilly, the people on the jetty are wearing coats and jackets. There's still nothing going on on the Havel. But the sun is shining.

What's missing is the cold beer.

Finally on the water. I can't remember what course we took. There was certainly

no boredom on board. I still don't know what Friedel is doing there. I think he's drizzling schnapps into the beer or pulling out an insect. Yes, Friedel can't take a joke when it comes to beer.

Friedel has plenty of Stubbis and sings a song. Maybe "Eine Seefahrt, die ist lustig".

So we sail along, feeling good, only we weren't fathers.

I can't remember how the day ended. I'm sure we packed everything up again, including the empty crate of beer. Fiedel and I probably went to our respective fiancées. They must have been happy about our beer flag.

I then married Monika W., a telecommunications assistant, on September 22. I sold the Inka S to Peter K., but not the Johnson. Instead, I got a real inflatable boat, bigger with a solid floor and windshield. Decades later, I once drove around Sanssouci in a Kremser as a father with the family.

Via Hamburg to Heidelberg

As a newly married couple from West Berlin, we also wanted to get out - through the "zone" to West Germany. Although the Eastern treaties had already been signed and the transit agreement was in force, transit through the GDR was still strange. And why not get to know West Germany - from the north to the center. The route went via Hamburg to St. Peter-Ording, then via Lohr am Main to Heidelberg. I've been to all of these destinations at one time or another. But more about that later.

We probably always drove to Hamburg via the Staaken border crossing on the B5, there was no highway back then. Monika is standing on the Binnenalster, not far from the Jungfernstieg, the town hall and the Michel from St. Pauli greets us.

And if you're already in Hamburg, head up to the Reeperbahn. We went to a transvestite show, which was something sinful back then. Next door was Café Keese (see the illuminated façade), which was always a ladies' club. Later we walked through Große Freiheit, which was even more sinful.

And if you're already in Hamburg, head up to the Reeperbahn. We went to a transvestite show, which was something sinful back then. Next door was Café Keese (see the illuminated façade), which was always a ladies' club. Later we walked through Große Freiheit, which was even more sinful.

I rode this moped from West Berlin to Hamburg at the end of the 1950s, just wearing a jacket for the weekend. I left on Friday evening and was back later on Sunday. The model can do a maximum of 45 km per hour, so at 300 km it took 7 to 8 hours (one trip). Sporty, isn't it?

We continued north to Stankt Peter-Ording - where the waves hit the beach. The town is located on the Eidelstedt peninsula and has endless 2 km wide beaches. You can also drive up there by car. However, you must not get in the way of a windsailor, which is a sailor on wheels. They really speed off.

It was too cold to swim and the wind was whistling around our ears. We stayed in one of the typical guesthouses. Thank goodness we were married, otherwise we would have had to stay in single rooms. Nah - and we really showed off my car. A two-tone Karmann Ghia 1600 wasn't available that often, not even in West Germany.

I went to St. Peter-Ording in this VW Beetle (Standard model) at the beginning of the 1960s. It was my first car, but Roswitha, who was with me, was not my first girlfriend. The Standard Beetle still had cable brakes, a non-synchronized gearbox, but already had indicators instead of turn signals and no split rear window. The color was matt gray, as were the hubcaps and the bumpers, and there were no trim strips. In other words, a simple car.

Then we left the windy north and drove southwest to the Main, more precisely to Lohr am Mainz in Lower Franconia. Why there of all places? At the beginning of the 1960s, the metalworkers' union sent me there for further training as a union shop steward. And because it was so nice, I wanted to show my

young wife this training center. The union secretary in charge was happy to do so. The small town is also well worth a visit.

My first flying experience is connected with the IGM training course in Lohr am Main. I flew from Berlin-Tempelhof to Frankfurt am Main in the old DC 4 Skymaster. It took a good hour and a half. And I got sick, and how, the whole bag was full. I flew back on the new Super Constellation from PanAm. It took less time and flew much more smoothly.

The next destination was Mespelbrunn moated castle. This is on the way to Heidelberg. Mespelbrunn Castle is located in a secluded Spessart valley between Frankfurt am Main and Würzburg. Among other things, it is known as the filming location for "Wirtshaus im Spessart" with Liselotte Pulver and Carlos Thompson and as the setting for the play of the same name.

Due to its hidden location, the castle survived all wars unscathed and has been preserved in its original form. It is still privately owned today. Since the early 1950s, the owners have been committed to preserving the castle as a monument and at the same time making it accessible to the general public.

I have enlarged the document on display. With some effort, you can decipher what happened after 1800. The note "the considerable robberies and violent

thefts committed by unknown persons during the last years in the Kingdom of Württemberg (by Napoleon's degrees, own remark)...." provides information. For example, the crimes are listed under the signal emblems of robbers and thieves.

Once we have established the link between the place and the events of the time, we can see that it was not wrong to set the robbery story there.

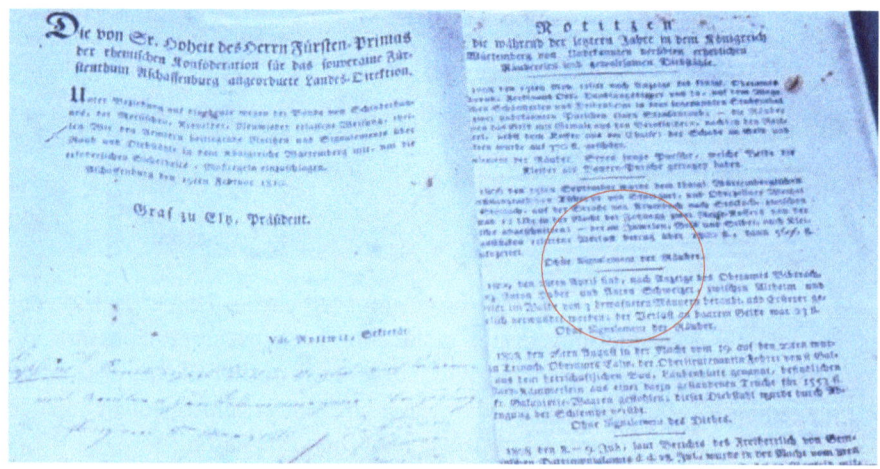

In the 60´s

The last stop on our journey also has something to do with the French. During the War of Succession, Heidelberg Castle was blown up by the troops of the Sun King. Since then, it has stood as a romantic ruin. There is so much to tell about the castle that you could fill pages with it. The story of the Great Barrel and its guardian may come to mind when you see the figure of Perkeo. The Elector's court jester pretended to be able to drink the whole barrel. The dwarf is said to have said: "Perché no?". This is where the name came from. You don't have to walk up to the castle, there is a funicular.

What else was there to see in Heidelberg? Perhaps the Alter Brücke bridge over the Neckar with its towers and Alt-Heidelberg with its historic student pubs. The Wirtshaus zum Seppl is as much a part of it as the castle or the Old Bridge. As early as the late 17th century, students and citizens would meet here over a convivial pint of beer. Years later, I stopped in there on a business trip.

The local fire department was on duty, with helmets and red fire engines in front of the church dedicated to the Holy Spirit on Heidelberg's market square. And the young couple sat on the parapet of the Old Bridges, already thinking about their way home: Frankfurt am Main, Kassel, Helmstedt, Transit, Dreilinden, West Berlin.

Good Skiing on the Teufelsberg and Good Hunting in the Jagdschloss (hunting lodge)

It was one of the cold winters in Berlin in the mid-60s. Minus 20 degrees were not uncommon in Berlin. With lots of snow, every year. In terms of winter sports, West Berliners were better off than those in the East. Because there was the Teufelsberg in Grunewald, actually a pile of rubble, 120 meters high, the second-highest elevation, all artificial. At the top you had a wonderful panoramic view. The picture shows the view towards the Olympic Stadium, further to the right is the Corbusierhaus, also known as the Wohnmaschine because of the 530 apartments (including the post office).

You won't believe it, there was first a toboggan run and later a proper ski slope. A toboggan run was nothing new, you could toboggan down the Insulaner

(another pile of rubble, but only half as high) or up the Kreuzberg, near where I lived. But a ski slope with a lift and everything that goes with it was quite something, even for West Berliners.

The Americans ran a radar station at the top of the Teufelsberg. So they always knew what was coming from Moscow. It was astonishing that nobody noticed how much the Cold War and sporting fun went hand in hand. Nowadays, guided tours are offered (with torches and such), there are concerts in the radar domes (because of the special sound) and a large street art gallery. But the best thing is the magnificent panoramic view.

Further south, not far from Teufelsberg, is the hunting lodge of the same name on Grunewaldsee. And as it was a beautiful winter's day, I went there with my fiancée Monika. The Hubertus hunts of the Hohenzollerns were long gone, but it was used as a backdrop for filming the Edgar Wallace movie.

It was one of the coldest winters in Berlin and yet so beautiful that you could go on

excursions. Even looking at the back of his fiancée was a pleasure.

Party or couples' get-together?

Yes, that's how people celebrated fifty years ago. I can't remember what or where. I would now like to describe the four couples in more detail. Because I don't want to push myself into the foreground, I'll start with the young woman on the right, who is mischievously turning away. This is Helga Seidlitzki, the first wife of my school friend Volker. He has put his arm around her shoulders and you can see her wedding ring shining. The young man on the left is Friedel Platte. He has already attracted his partner. She didn't become his wife later. Friedel studied mechanical engineering with me at the Beuth Engineering Academy. I can't remember the names of the couple in the middle. They were married, I know that, and he also went to night school at Beuth. He had a good laugh here, but he had a hard time there. How often Friedel and I practiced with him. The blonde woman sitting there so elegantly was newly married to me. And finally me, with my arm around Monika.

They were all dressed up. The ladies in glittering dresses or little black dresses, the men in suits with white shirts and slim ties. The hairstyles ranged from conventional to loose. On the coffee table, lots of glasses and stubbis, the 0.33-liter beer bottles. Beer was rationally drunk from the bottle, the Stubbis were so handy. Friedel is just checking to see if there's any of the Schultheiß Pils left.

And his partner's arm just happens to be resting on his thigh. Certainly not intentional.

Party or couples' get-together? Nowadays, a party would mean something different, it would also include singles. And a couple's get-together? What do the two young ladies think? Perhaps that their husbands have moved on in their careers. That could also have been the reason for the party. The get-together was certainly a happy one.

In the 70´s

Farewell to grandma at the heath cemetery

This is not intended to be a sad story, but rather to show how people come and go. My grandma had me in her care and never wanted me to live with my stepfather. She copied the song from the "...wieviel Sternlein stehen" and you can see the document here. It was probably written in the fifties of the last century. She loved the little blond boy very much. The writing is remarkable, written with a fountain pen. It's not actually a woman's handwriting and, as we learned before the First World War, it's in Latin script. We write in this script again today, hardly anyone can write in Sütterlin anymore.

In the 70's

Later on, my grandmother was no longer able to write, due to gout. The illness had left her bedridden and Grandpa had to look after her. Only from his pension, there was no care insurance yet. And at some point it was no longer possible. She died on August 30, 1974. At the age of just 73. The urn burial took place at the Heidefriedhof cemetery in Berlin-Tempelhof.

Grandpa said goodbye to his wife, with whom he had celebrated his golden wedding anniversary not so long ago. Behind them are my cousin Christiane and me. Then her parents and the other mourners. I think my cousin Wolfgang was also there. The second picture shows my aunt Ilse Mundt next to her father. I'm the next to say goodbye. Yes, the little boy has grown up.

Many of the people in the pictures are no longer alive, including my mother, who probably took the photos.

Grandpa died five years later at the age of 88. We, Gunhild and I, had often looked for him in Berlin. Grandpa's urn was buried next to his wife's. The gravestone stands in its place after 46 years, the resting period has been over for ages. *

Not just one, but two people have gone. One too soon, the other at an advanced age. I'm sure they would have been happy to see their great-granddaughter. And can little Julie sing the song of the little star?

I now have the gravestone in my garden. I took it with me from Berlin. When I walk past it, I can remember my grandparents.

Joachim wants to go sailing with me on Sunday

I haven't found a better title than that of the old hit. And please don't equate Joachim with the original lyrics. In any case, I don't know anything about it.

In the 70´s

Whether he always wanted to sail with me is another matter. I knew Joachim G. from Berlin College. He had trained as an agricultural machinery mechanic and worked on them in Australia. He was excluded from English lessons. He was fluent in English. It was only the female connection that didn't really work out. More about that and other things later.

Now to me and sailing. It must have been around the beginning of the 1970s when I needed a sailing boat and I bought a 420 dinghy, actually a youth sports boat of French origin with a sail area of 12.5 m². I first learned to sail by doing, later in a sailing course at the university sports department. It was only a few years ago that I learned to sail a sports boat. Our sailing area was the Lower Havel. I found a parking space for my boat and trailer at the Keser boat center

in Pichelswerder. The boat had to be slipped in and paddled to the mouth of the Havel, about 800 meters. Downstream, that's downstream, it was fine and setting a bit of headsail helped, but upstream on the Havel, you had to make an effort. With Joachim it was fine, with young ladies on board less so.

Before reaching the mouth of the Havel, we set sail on command: "Jib or main ahead!" On good days, we cruised until shortly before Potsdam, always along the zonal border. Commands: "Clear to tack - It's clear - Headsail back - Ree!" "Or clear to jibe - sheets off - round astern! "Only that with the Stubbis (0.33 l beer bottles) went all by itself. After sailing, we went to the Greek restaurant on Kurfürstendamm. Souvlaki and a nice big Helles. That's how it went from start to finish, year after year. At some point, Joachim got fed up with being in command and gave up his job as foresailor. I then sold the boat to my fellow

business student Klaus Schätte. He would have been better off getting his sailing license.

I met Joachim from time to time later on. He had dropped out of his economics degree at the FU, it was too capitalistic for him. He changed subjects and went to work for the municipal theaters as a stage fitter and scenery pusher. As far as I know, he later lived in Weddig.

I have fond memories of those wonderful times on the water.

Off to Seven Sisters

What on earth motivated Annette and Hans C and their son Ilya to rent a vacation apartment in a coal mine nest in South Wales? I can't remember Annette's later interview with the local newspaper about it. In any case, there are cozier places in the world than this. The wool from the sheep on the coal heaps no longer needed to be dyed black and the fish and chips were served in their original packaging (yesterday's newspaper). There was also still plenty of fuel (cooking oil) to be obtained and the neighbors ensured the supply of carrots. Perhaps they were intended for the sheep (or goats).

At the time I was friends with Gunhild, now my sister-in-law.

Somehow the destination appealed to us, especially as we were able to see London and Winsor on the way there. And we were also looking forward to

seeing the C. again. We did one together. But more about that later.

On the way to Seven Sisters, the car went on strike in Swansea, three quarters of an hour from our destination. We knew the VW garage from a previous breakdown (new engine in the VW Beetle). We were towed in and the fault was quickly rectified (just a new ignition distributor). Finally we had arrived. The picture shows that sticking out the tongue was probably very fashionable at the end of the seventies of the last century, other pictures also show this.

It's not far from Seven Sisters to the coast and the beaches. I have no idea what we did there, apart from going for a walk and Ilya digging up half the beach. Swimming was not on the agenda. Oh yes, I just remembered that I bought a small secretary at the antique market in Swansea.

Our trip to the Gower Peninsula (Gower Area of Outstanding Natural Beauty) was remarkable. It was great: the view, the waves, the cliffs. Gunhild's red trousers fit so wonderfully into the picture.

From memory, I can say that it was a nice vacation. On the way back on the ferry, I met my friend from the evening school for technicians, Friedel Platte, with the girl he'd been entrusted with. Or was that another time? In any case, the sheep from the coal heap greeted me one last time.

In the 70´s

The silver Beetle

I bought the silver Beetle towards the end of my studies in 1974. This model already had 44 hp compared to the "normal" 30 hp. I had got a good job through TUSMA (TU students do everything) and could afford this vehicle. In the picture, it is parked in front of the entrance to Dudenstraße 11 (see arrow). My school friend Volker lived there in the rear building, as did Sigrid in the Wannsee photo (in the front building).

I lived in the corner house, Burgherrenstraße 11, with grandma and grandpa for almost 30 years. On the 4th floor, where the balcony door is open. Our cat once fell from up there and survived the fall with a broken leg. The house was built in 1910 and already had an elevator, which also worked in later years, and a servants' entrance with stairs leading to the kitchens. The non-servants lived in the side wing. The house was not painted until 1970.

In the 70´s

In the next picture, you can see my grandfather Alfred B. standing next to Solveig's godmother Gunhild at the aforementioned Beetle. The photo was taken a little later. Granddad was already over 85 and was still bouncing around. Gunhild was still in her twenties and was also a friend of mine. She already knew my grandfather from several visits to Berlin. In the background you can see parts of the Tempelhof Central Airport complex. The big yellow (19 bus) with the beer advertisement is just stopping at the airport subway station. Just behind it is the airlift memorial, known to Berliners as the "Hungerkralle". John F. Kennedy also landed at this airport shortly after the Wall was built in 1961. The American president drove openly along Dudenstraße here with the

governing mayor Willy Brandt and the Federal Chancellor Konrad Adenauer. We waved to them from the balcony. We headed towards Schöneberg Town Hall, where Kennedy gave the famous speech. We all still remember one sentence from it today.

In the last picture, the Beetle is there again, only no longer in Berlin-Tempelhof, but in Frohacker in Ockenfels, a local community of Linz am Rhein. I lived there with Gunhild, who was training as a dental technician in Kasbach. We had moved into the lower apartment. I then found a new job in Wiesbaden, the silver Beetle came with me, but not Gunhild.

***

Personal details from Kurfürstendamm

So much for the topic

Last night I watched another program on ARD about mysterious places. This time it was the boulevard Kurfürstendamm, known to Berliners as Kudamm for short. The program showed the eventful history of the boulevard. Anyone can read, watch and listen to the podcast. Instead, I came up with the idea of writing down how Kurfürstendamm has affected me personally, what I have experienced there from the 1950s to the present day. It doesn't reveal anything mysterious, but it does subliminally reveal a lot of zeitgeist and attitude to life.

Staple blues and rock and roll

"He'll Have to Go" is an American country and pop hit that came out in October 1959, the performer was the legendary Jim Reeves. Here is a picture of him and the first verse of the song:

> Put your sweet lips a little closer to the phone
>
> Let's pretend that we're together, all alone
>
> I'll tell the man to turn the jukebox way down low
>
> And you can tell your friend there with you he'll have to go

When I was eighteen, I often went to the Kudamm and squeezed into "Asia". It was a dance club at the top end of the boulevards. Much of it was still in ruins. The music came from the jukebox. When this hit came on, it got dim and the couples danced close together, as if clinging to each other. People from Cologne would say: "I'm in, that's great!"

I was also there when Bill Haley came on with the famous "Rock around the Clock". The rock and roll was quite demanding. I still enjoyed dancing to it later.

Don't take it so much to heart - Let it be

This song came to mind when I went to the Kudamm early in the morning towards the end of my studies. It was a beautiful May Sunday and my car was parked on the central reservation. The night had been short, but very lively. And I didn't take the whole thing to heart. Here is the piano score of the catchy Beatles song. For the titles, I chose the German translation of the song, "Lass es geschehen" would be more literal.

Personal details from Kurfürstendamm

The whale at the Europa-Center

It was in the 50s. On Breitscheidplatz, the Kaiser Wilhelm Memorial Church stood in ruins. The Eiermann buildings were added much later. The Kudamm begins at Breitscheidplatz on one side and Tauentzien with the KADEWE on the other.

Right there on the corner (see picture) there was a whale exhibition. All of West Berlin marveled at the large dead animal, possibly a blue whale. And the Berliners also learned something about whaling and whale processing. Today, the globe fountain stands there, disrespectfully called "Wasserklops" by Berliners.

The Europa-Center was added in the 1960s. It had a gallery at a height of 86 meters from which you could look out over the Kudamm. I think the first Daitokai was established under the gallery. I went there a few times with Monika. We ate sukiyaki (jap. 鋤焼 or すき焼き) and drank sake (jap. 酒) with it, and enjoyed the beautiful view of Kurfürstendamm. But that was back in the 70s. If you ignore the "Upper West" high-rise and the Waldorf-Astoria luxury hotel. The photo roughly reflects the view at that time.

Let's twist again

"Come on let's twist again like we did last summer." That was a song by Chubby Checker from 1961. A dance on the spot. No more of the wild drums of rock and roll. Twist wasn't danced just anywhere, but at the New Eden on Kurfürstendamm, with Peter and Renate and other friends. Unfortunately, I couldn't clearly identify the New Eden in any of the pictures, but I did find a picture of the Old Eden. Later, there was also the Big Eden, which was sold by the subsequent owner Rolf Eden in 2006.

Personal details from Kurfürstendamm

I remember one Saturday evening when Monika and I were in the New Eden Twisten. We had parked the car on the central reservation on the Kudamm. On the way back to the car, it was raining cats and dogs. We made ourselves comfortable first, because the top was closed. Later, I had to crank the engine, as the MGA was very sensitive to rain. That's why a crank rod was part of the basic accessories.

Flower job on Kurfürstendamm - a fiasco

I looked for an apprenticeship straight after leaving school. In the meantime, I wanted to earn some money as a flower delivery boy in a store on the Kudamm. I was also supposed to help out in the store. The flower store was not far from the MGM movie theater, which no longer exists today. It could have been here.

So I got on my bike and delivered the bouquets. Sometimes there was no one there and I brought them back, which didn't make the bouquets any better. Then my bike was stolen and I had to travel by bus and train, which was even worse for the flowers. So I lost my job as well as my bike. What a fiasco!

A fiasco is the term used to describe a failure. In Italian, fiasco originally and still today refers to a big-bellied wine bottle. The word is related to the German word "Flasche". I was one of those, I mean flowery.

Personal details from Kurfürstendamm

Clothing and a fatal appointment

I started the 2nd educational path in 1968. Before that, Monika and I had earned a good living. The expensive sports car had been sold and I had made pretty watering cans and birdcages in the Klewer Art Studio for piecework. So we had

money left over for trendy clothes. These were available in the boutiques on Kurfürstendamm, for example in one for young men's fashion on the corner of Schlüterstraße. I'll come back to this place later. Back then, I used to buy suits with vests in size 102 or 106 (the size for tall and slim men). Today, I'm a normal men's size 54 and a size 38 was appropriate for Monika. The Coco Chanel-style costumes looked good on her. The picture shows the two of us on a trip to Bruges (beguinage).

ow to the fatal date. As a student, I went on a date with Magret at this point. We'd been together for a while and we'd done a lot together: we'd driven her around as a Christmas angel, sold her old sailing yacht, been to Rome with her on New Year's Eve. We just didn't have any prospects together, especially as she had a 10-year-old daughter who often stayed with her grandmother in Celle.

Personal details from Kurfürstendamm

The lack of prospects for a family was probably the reason why I met her at the meeting point with an established gentleman. She had probably met him through a marriage advertisement. That made me gulp. That wouldn't have happened with a cell phone, but they didn't exist back then. We went to a Spanish restaurant, which was actually where I wanted to go. But I sneaked out after a glass of Rioja. I wonder what happened to it. It didn't fit behind and in front.

I am so homesick for the Kurfürstendamm - Boulevard in festive splendor

I visited my friend Hans and his wife Annette a few times before Christmas. I also tried to reach my old friend Peter and his wife Renate, as well as my cousin Christiane. When I landed at Tegel, I took the airport bus to Zoo station and changed to the 110 bus. It went all the way along the boulevard towards Zehlendorf, where my overnight accommodation was waiting. 3,600 m of festive splendor, which was particularly good to admire in the double-decker up front.

I remembered the song by Hildegard Knef: "Ich so Heimweh nach dem Kurfürstendamm" from 1964, but it may be older. Here is the first verse:

Personal details from Kurfürstendamm

I'm so homesick for the Kurfürstendamm,

I'm so longing for my Berlin!

And do I also see in Frankfurt, Munich, Hamburg or Vienna

People make an effort, but Berlin remains Berlin.

I'm so homesick for the Kurfürstendamm,

Berlin speed, bustle and fuss!

In German

Ich hab so Heimweh nach dem Kurfürstendamm,

Hab so Sehnsucht nach meinem Berlin!

Und seh ich auch in Frankfurt, München, Hamburg oder Wien

Die Leute sich bemühn, Berlin bleibt doch Berlin.

Ich hab so Heimweh nach dem Kurfürstendamm,

Berliner Tempo, Betrieb und Tamtam!

The verse ends with: *If I had an apartment somewhere, no matter how new it was, I'll stay true to Berlin, my old love!* Quite sentimental. You can get sentimental at this sight.

Personal details from Kurfürstendamm

Opposite the Kranzlereck and more than 36 degrees Celsius in the shade

Last year we were in Berlin to visit the Fontane exhibition in Neuruppin with Hans and Annette. We stayed centrally on Kurfürstendamm at the Hotel Azimut. Here is the description:

The modern AZIMUT Hotel Berlin Kurfürstendamm in the heart of Berlin is located in two historic buildings from the early 20th century. It is located directly on Kurfürstendamm, the 125-year-old and world-famous boulevard from the imperial era and is only a few minutes' walk from the Memorial Church.

Well - our "modern" room had no air conditioning, but thick curtains to keep out the sun's heat. But they couldn't do that on one of the hottest days in Berlin. At least there was a fan and at night we opened the windows, which didn't make things any better as the traffic noise was enormous. Every few minutes a bus rolled past the windows on the second floor. But no more complaining.

As we didn't want to have breakfast in the hotel, we looked for and found a breakfast bakery in the "Neue Kranzlereck". No more Café Kranzler, as the historic coffee house closed in 2000. For the sake of nostalgia, here is a picture of the old Kranzlereck, and now the new one with the Berlin Bear Quadriga.

Personal details from Kurfürstendamm

For our late afternoon departure, we took the airport bus to Tegel. And we were lucky: the plane made a loop over Berlin illuminated in the evening, the Kudamm with its lights clearly visible.

Our friend Annette is still raving about the beautiful day in Neuruppin.

"… and in the evening we stroll home along the Kudamm." From the song "Little Girl from Berlin" by Chris Howland.

„… und am Abend bummeln wir übern Kudamm dann nach Haus." Aus dem Lied „Kleines Mädchen von Berlin" von Chris Howland.

Personal details from Kurfürstendamm

Set theory with the Berlin clock

On the corner of Kudamm and Uhlandstraße stood the Berlin Clock, also known as the "Mengenlehreuhr". This was a public clock that was developed in 1975 by Dieter Binninger on behalf of the Berlin Senate and displayed the time using a number of illuminated lamps.

The clock has nothing to do with set theory. Here is an explanation of its function:

The time is displayed in a place value system to the base of 5. The hours and minutes are shown by illuminated segments in four strips arranged horizontally one below the other. There are four lights in the first, second and fourth lines and eleven in the third. The first two lines show the hour with red lights, with one illuminated segment in the upper strip representing five hours and one in the lower strip representing one hour. The current hour results from the addition of the values. Accordingly, the minutes are displayed in the two lower lines with yellow segments in steps of five and one. The lights for 15, 30 and 45 minutes are red to make them easier to read. Above the lines there is a round flashing light that is switched on or off every second.

Understand everything? The light consumption was enormous and cost the city council DM 5,000 a year. The clock was therefore taken out of service in 1995. This would not have happened with today's LEDs. Sponsored by the business people, it now stands somewhat apart in front of the tourist information office on Budapester Straße.

I "visited" the clock at its old location as part of a motorcycle trip to Berlin. Would you like to see which model* I rode, i.e. cruised, along the Kudamm?

*Harley-Davidson Electra Glide FLHS Touring Sport

Que voulez-vous manger, s'il vous plaît - in the Maison de France

On April 21, 1950, the French city commander General Jean Ganeval and Lord Mayor Ernst Reuter ("Look at this city...") opened the new cultural center as a Franco-German meeting place "Maison de France" at Kurfürstendamm 211. There was the Institut francais Berlin, the Cinema Paris and a French restaurant on the 4th floor.

Monika and I were devilishly taken with the French restaurant. We thought it was totally chic. I can still remember two things: Monika's outfit and the order. The 60s can be associated with leather clothing, not just jackets and pants, but also miniskirts with vests. Monika was wearing something like that in black. Totally fashionable! When we ordered, the waiter advised us against the inexpensive dishes. Coq au vin is a French culinary classic, but there are better things. We went for the better one. We also didn't have to concentrate on

Personal details from Kurfürstendamm

French. I didn't have a second foreign language at school, English was hard enough. Monika was actually quite good at French, she had the "Quali", but didn't dare. We didn't go to the cinema and I don't know if the movies were subtitled.

The Maison de France was also booming, as it often was on the Kudamm. On

August 25, 1983, there was a bomb attack on the building. With one dead. The Stasi had a hand in it.

The Maison de France was reopened two years later. The old restaurant no longer exists, but a new one has opened, the restaurant "Brasserie Le Paris" on the ground floor facing the street. I will be visiting that soon.

Personal details from Kurfürstendamm

Bowling course on Kurfürstendamm

My studies were slowly coming to an end, I had to pass the preliminary exams in ABWL and SBWL (General Business Administration and Special Business Administration). After all, they were a prerequisite for the diploma examination. Anyone with a grade of at least 4.3 was lucky. The notice with matriculation number and grade 5.0 was long and longer. My fellow student and friend Klaus probably didn't cram often and was one of the unfortunate ones. He also had other things on his mind: for example, how to get a free bowling course. It took place at the bowling center on Lehniner Platz, a venue that no longer exists. So we bowled for free. Then our heads were free to study again. Klaus was also to be envied for his good figure when he was an extra in the musical "Hair" at the Theater des Westens. And he eventually became a business graduate too.

"Because the old are sleeping, the young have to run"* - ...and who controls the traffic

Two days after the assassination attempt on Rudi Dutschke, there was a demonstration on Kurfürstendamm on Good Friday, April 13, 1968. The Socialist German Student Union (SDS) called for this march. SDS was part of the West German Extra-Parliamentary Opposition (APO). Over 2,000 demonstrators made their way from Lehniner Platz to the Memorial Church. The demonstrators were mainly young people. They demanded an hour of airtime every day.

Personal details from Kurfürstendamm

I have to admit, I wasn't there. I wanted to become a student and was still very much in the middle-class camp. In the eyes of the demonstrators at the time, it sounded like this: "If you sleep with the same person twice, you're already part of the establishment"**. Where might the picture have been taken from? I mean from the traffic pulpit on the corner of Kudamm and Joachimsthaler Straße. You could regulate traffic from a higher vantage point from the pulpit. There is still a kiosk under the pavilion roof and access to the subway. The public toilets and telephones have been renovated.

Translation:

* „Weil die Alten pennen, müssen Junge rennen"

** „Wer zweimal mit derselben pennt, gehört schon zum Establishment"

Bleistreu - Mykonos - Paris Bar - Zwiebelfisch - Loretta im Garten - pleasure and crime, all not far from Kurfürstendamm

I loved going to Café Bleibtreu. I usually met up with Klaus and Karin for one or more beers. We called it Café Bleistreu because on June 27, 1970, an armed gang commissioned by brothel owner Hans Helmcke attacked competing Iranian pimps at the Bucharest restaurant, killing one of them and injuring three others. In reference to this shooting, Bleibtreustraße was also known for a long time as "Bleistreu-Straße" in the Berlin vernacular.

I think it was Mykonos, where I used to meet my friends, usually with Renate. The routine was always the same: soulaki for me and tzatziki for the others, plenty of retsina for everyone, then mavrodaphne on top and uozo afterwards. It wasn't always this moist and joyful.

The assassination attempt on September 17, 1992 became known as the Mykonos assassination. Four Iranian-Kurdish politicians in exile were shot dead in this pub in Prager Straße in Berlin-Wilmersdorf on behalf of the Iranian secret service, and another customer and the landlord were seriously injured.

It was known as the Berlin salon of the beautiful and wild, the rich and clever - the legendary "Paris Bar". I was a guest a few times and did not have the above-mentioned characteristics. I still remember Otto Schily, whom I sat opposite not far away. He was a regular here, but probably not yet Federal

Personal details from Kurfürstendamm

Minister of the Interior. It was a swan song for an institution when the Paris Bar unexpectedly filed for bankruptcy. Somehow the bar continued to operate, even if some of the guests were curious tourists. But perhaps the old glory will return.

I wanted to stop off at Zwiebelfisch recently, I've been there from time to time. It was packed, no room for an older person. The Zwiebelfisch was known as a student pub, as well as an old 68ers' pub. I've never heard this term before, but I really like it.

For others, it is a meeting place for celebrities and Charlottenburg bohemians. In any case, the restaurant is a Berlin institution. Now it has had to close. As reported, unknown persons had set fire to the back wall of the Zwiebelfisch on 21.03.2020. The flames engulfed the restaurant and burned parts of the interior. A donation account has now been set up.

In the 1970s, Loretta im Garten was the largest and best-known beer garden in Berlin, right next to Kudamm on Lietzenburger Straße. In a 10,000 square meter gap between buildings, the beer garden offered 3,000 seats, a mini Ferris wheel at the entrance, a children's playground and a beach volleyball court. It was always busy and a great place to meet up with friends. I

went there a few times with my friend Magret and her daughter. It was a great place for the child to play and for me to enjoy a beer. Today there are two beer gardens in Berlin,

Loretta an der Spree and Loretta am Wannsee, where I recently had a nice break with my wife and daughter.

What remains - a look back at experiences

Television went in search of clues, showing the rise and fall, the glittering world and the dark side of the notorious boulevard. They told of criminal cases, the assassination attempt on Rudi Dutschke and the Kurfürstendamm as a place of longing. I wrote down what I experienced on and around the Kudamm. Very personal things, in small pieces. I don't associate this so much with memories from my younger years, rather it was nice to let things happen again. Later in life, I never found a place with so much appeal. Perhaps the song by Hildegard Knef from 1963 also fits in with this:

Berlin, your face has freckles And your mouth is much too big Your silver eyes are undaunted But you never say: "What am I doing?"	Berlin, dein Gesicht hat Sommersprossen Und dein Mund ist viel zu groß Dein Silberblick ist unverdrossen Doch nie sagst du: „Was mach' ich bloß?"

***

Student Christmas stories

The head Santa Claus from the bench

At around five o'clock on Christmas Eve, I, already an engineering candidate, was sitting in front of the telephone in the offices of the Student Employment Service of the Technical University (TUSMA) in Hardenbergstraße. Hans C. didn't fancy the job this time and let me have a go.

"So listen, Santa wanted to come half an hour ago, the children are waiting!" It went on and on like that.

"Call again if there's no one at the door in a quarter of an hour." Luckily, I had some Christmas friends in reserve. And a few more who were waiting for additional orders.

Some of the foreign fellow students in Santa Claus costumes weren't up to the well-intentioned nip - ten visits can add up to a lot. But there were also professionals. I remember one tall business student who was still standing up straight after 12 "Hohohoho, here I am".

By ten in the evening, the whole thing was over. The stress over a beer in your favorite pub was forgotten. "Merry Christmas!"

Excerpt from Wikipedia/ TUSMA

Special placement TUSMA Santa Claus campaign

TUSMA's student Santas and angels, who were placed before Christmas, were particularly well known. From 2000 until the end of TUSMA, the Santas worked together with the Heinzelmännchen as "Berlin Santa Claus" and delivered presents to up to 10,000 Berlin families at peak times at Christmas.

TUSMA was financed exclusively by the commissions of the registered students, while the Heinzelmännchen **(Brownies)** *were funded by the Studentenwerk. The TUSMA Santa Claus campaign in particular was organized by a group of students who actively and creatively supported the TUSMA-financed "head Santa Claus" with unpaid telephone services. The success of this concept was demonstrated by the fact that the Santa Claus campaign still had more orders when TUSMA's advertising resources for the Santa Claus campaign had to be drastically cut back and only the Heinzelmännchen were left to put up posters around the city. After German reunification, the number of orders for the Santa Claus campaign increased to such an extent that paid student telephone staff had to be employed for the first time. These were financed by the increased* *commissions paid to the students. The TUSMA Santa Claus campaign was also the first to place Christmas angels accompanied by Santas again after a long break. The Heinzelmännchen did not follow suit until years later. After internal disputes, a former TUSMA student spun off the Berlin Santa Claus Center in 2004, which enabled all citizens to appear as Santa Claus and Santa Claus angels on Christmas Eve in Berlin and the surrounding area, regardless of their student status. The first members of the Berlin Santa Claus Center were largely drawn from the pool of former TUSMA and Heinzelmännchen Santa Clauses who wanted to continue doing this work after their studies and were no longer allowed to do so at the student employment agencies.*

Chauffeur for the Christmas angel

It was already dark on Christmas Eve when I set off with the Christmas angel. My friend Magret, all in white with wings and a wreath of stars, was working as a Christmas angel on behalf of the student employment agency TUSMA. Students at the University of Education could also take advantage of this. Magret was enrolled there.

At that time, Christmas angels were still rare at TUSMA (TU students do everything), which was probably also due to the large male student body. It was a different story with the competition from the FU, Die Heinzelmännchen. This was probably due to the large proportion of female students. So - the conservative Berlin household preferred Santa Claus from TUSMA.

TUSMA's logistics department had staked out the claims for the gnomes, think of the smaller foreign students, and angels in a tight radius. So the 10 to 12 visits took about two hours. Good money plus tips and/or schnapps.

Afterwards we visited grandma and grandpa, who were very happy about the Christmas angel. Then there was a Christmas party at Magret's friend's. "Merry Christmas!"

We continued our get-together. First to Celle, where her mother lived, and then from Hanover on the night train to Rome. A German teacher training course was taking place in the Domus Pacis Roma. Those were wonderful days between the years.

Student Christmas stories

Delicate as marzipan

It was shortly before Christmas Eve when we, myself, Hans C.i and another colleague, went to work as temporary staff in a large supermarket in Berlin-Lichterfelde. We got the job through the TU's student employment agency (TUSMA). We were still at the Berlin-Kolleg to get the necessary qualifications and someone had found out that we could get work through TUSMA.

So we made ourselves useful. It started with pricing the goods and ended with unloading Christmas trees and crates of beer. The store manager took a special liking to me. I was allowed to sell Christmas geese, frozen and very fresh from Poland. You have to know that Berliners love Christmas poultry from Poland.

The Polish geese were "as tender as marzipan" and sold like hot cakes. If the comparison hangs a little. The frozen ones were more work, especially as the storage location was hellishly cold and the geese were as hard as stone. This comparison hangs even deeper. The pieces of ice cream were weighed and sold by the kilo. I loved the "marzipan geese" more.

Hans C., on the other hand, had the "dream job". He sold "Berliner Kindl" beer in Stubbis (0.33 l bottles) by the crate. He did this outside, when the temperatures were still above zero. In the evening, all the beer had to go into the warm, several pallets. Now, he wasn't quite so good at handling pallet trucks, called "Eidechse" (lizard), so he sometimes dropped a crate. Maybe it was too slippery. We made a mess of the "damaged goods", because half crates were not sold. Cheers and "Merry Christmas!"

Student Christmas stories

The store manager didn't treat us to our well-earned refreshments and didn't sign the work sheets. But we made up for it at the head office between the years. The mood was good again, even though it was freezing cold in Berlin.

***

Advent fun

Go into the garden on St. Barbara's Day.

Go to the bare cherry tree and say:

Short is the day, gray is the time.

Winter is beginning, spring is far away.

But in three weeks, it will happen:

We'll celebrate a festival, like spring so beautiful.

Tree, give me a branch from you.

Even if it's bare, I'll take it with me:

And it will blossom in blissful splendor

in the middle of winter on Christmas Eve.

A well-known poem for St. Barbara's Day was written by the poet Josef Guggenmoos.

St. Barbara is known to be the patron saint of miners, but also of fireworkers, gunners and shipbuilders. They all celebrate St. Barbara's Day on December 4. So do the shipbuilding students at the Technical University of Berlin. The festivities took place in the old part of the university (see picture), right next to the modern main building, i.e. in the rooms of the old Königlich Technische Hochschule zu Berlin-Charlottenburg.

The party was a real insider tip among the students. There was always something going on. There were always nice people to meet. It's a shame that I only found out about it when I was a student. Advent can be fun that way.

Student Christmas stories

The main building seen from the side

A thoughtful Christmas present

It was probably just before Christmas. I had diligently completed my first semester of industrial engineering and was now in my second. The sister of my friend Hans Regine had made friends with me. Notice the order.

I picked her up for a Christmas party. By chance, we ran into Hans and his wife Annette. He was very surprised about this relationship. He didn't find it exciting. Regine gave me two glass beer mugs. One of them is on my desk and serves as a reservoir for used stamps, see picture. When the jar is full, I send the stamps to the stamp office in Bethel. Then they'll have something to do over Christmas.

When I look at the jar, I think about her life, which I was able to follow through her brother. Regine also studied philology at the TU Berlin. She then went to the Sorbonne and studied Romance languages and literature there. She once wrote to me from there. She met her future husband, a Syrian, in Paris.

She became a teacher in Berlin. Then her daughter Leonie was born, around the same time as my daughter Louise. The marriage broke up. Regine never remarried. Leonie studied music and lived with her girlfriend, an employee in the TU student office. Regine fell seriously ill and died. Last year we visited her at the Südfriedhof Stansdorf. We were actually only a couple for a few months. I should have visited her once when she was ill. But now I think of her when I look at the glass. Especially at Christmas.

Regine and I, in the look of the 70s, at a teacher training course in St. Andreasberg in the Harz Mountains, 1971

Dominoes

Dominoes for Christmas? Of course! For games and for eating. My little Christmas story is about the latter. To speed up production, Hans C. and I were commissioned by TUSMA to carry out development work on a domino-cutting machine in a metalworking workshop. The machine was supposed to cut the assembled domino slabs - gingerbread on the bottom, a layer of jelly on top and then a marzipan layer - into cubes, which were then coated with chocolate or icing.

"Let's play dumb", as we know from the Feuerzangenbowle. The machine should work like this: The cake slab is cut into strips by a rotating knife roller on a conveyor belt, then mechanically rotated through 90 degrees and cut back into cubes.

Hans did the turning work and I designed the mechanics. Now Hans is a trained machine fitter and "only" a state-certified mechanical engineer, but not in the design department, but in the operating technology department. The boss was satisfied with Hans' work, but less so with mine. I was then allowed to stop work. But the machine was already running on the belt and the knife roller. Whether the prototype was used in time for Christmas is beyond Hans' and my knowledge. But - we like to talk about it at Christmas time. Merry Christmas!

Volume II

Stories from West Germany and beyond

Preface to Volume II

Not all my stories are autobiographical and happened that way, the poems are not anyway and some exercises from the writing workshop simply did not allow that, although I have tried to come across as confident and life-affirming with my texts. Who wants to say negative things about their life? Of course, there was that too, but I based it on reality.

Furthermore, I didn't stick to the chronological sequence of events; the themes were more important to me. So I start with a reference to my home town and the Fräulein miracle, which I was able to experience myself.

The experiences on the water happened over the years with the length of the boats and ships. What has remained is my enjoyment of dinghies, sailing dinghies, motor cruisers and mega ships. I am thinking about starting a "cruise book".

My West German stories also include a reference to the city where our children grew up and their mother worked as a dentist. We're talking about Cologne, and what better place, apart from the Cologne Fastelovend (carnival), than to describe a tour of the breweries. We are doing four. Here, too, a book is in the making that deals with the "Stenzelberg Carnival", that much is revealed: It's a book for beginners and copycats.

There are reports about the visits in and around Berlin. Reports yes, and a story too. I can't answer why it mostly had to be castles and their conversions. Must be my Prussian nature.

The romantic trips are due to the female company. A boat trip here, a bike trip there, and then a car trip to the south. There's also a bit of regional studies.

There are texts from the writing workshop, which are actually writing exercises and have hopefully developed into something better over time. The last text summarizes what has been learned.

Three poems form the conclusion. I would describe them as age-appropriate. They were all written on cruises, which makes you think. I have supplemented this edition with two short stories and revised everything once again.

I have added my own photos to most of the stories, some of the pictures are taken from the Internet, some from literature. This makes it easier to imagine the stories. The pictures from the writing workshop are guidelines.

Preface to Volume II

The illustrated stories from West Germany are followed as a second book by those from West Berlin, where I spent the first half of my life.

My Fraulein

I want to be with you - my Fraulein

"Far across the big pond lives a daughter on the old Rhine, whom I loved and left, can't forget her, because I miss you so much, my pretty lady". This is how the first verse of this love song could be translated. Every night, when the stars rise, the admirer looks up into the sky. By the same stars he has sworn his love to the lady. He sees the face of the beloved woman before him, his abandoned sweetheart. He sees himself strolling hand in hand along the banks of the Rhine with the pretty young woman, gazing at the stars in love.

This is the love song of an American who was stationed in Germany as a GI and is now back in his homeland, thinking about his beloved. The song is set to a traditional country music style. Elongated fiddle, elongated vowels. The melody is borrowed from a Woody Guthrie song, the country icon of the 1930s. Country singer Bobby Helms made his debut with the song. The song remained in the US country charts for a year in 1957, even reaching number one for four weeks. Well-known country singers interpreted it in the following years, most recently in 2017. There are German versions of the song with an umlaut, and even a version with lyrics in Mandarin. Country singer Kitty Wells responded with the song "(I'll Always Be Your) Fraulein". This song also became a hit.

Why the Americans, and not only the Americans, liked the song so much can only be explained by a certain melancholy in the song. The restrained waltz beat, the ups and downs of the vocals with long vowels or just the lyrics, which come across as banal and longing. The country singer Bobby Helms later revealed his dark side when he learned from the newspaper that his Munich "Fraulein" had drowned herself in the Rhine after saying goodbye.

Perhaps it was the time. The American President Dwight D. Eisenhower, a war hero and of German descent, no longer appealed to young people; only the next U.S. President would do so with his New Frontier. So it was probably the servicemen who stuck by the general and still dreamed of their "frontline" service. The county scene is said to be conservative anyway.

The fascinating thing is probably the woman herself. The word is difficult for Americans to pronounce, so they dropped the *umlaut*. The form of address Fräulein was already considered unfashionable in the 60s. Fräulein in a double diminutive was mostly used by mothers to reprimand their pubescent daughters. So what were the GIs into with the young women? What was so different from home? The term "Fräuleinwunder", coined in the USA, stood for young, attractive, modern, self-confident and desirable women in post-war Germany. Well, if no one took the bait.

Little girl from Berlin

I only have you in mind

A love song from a divided city

It's not really clear who the love in the song is for, the little girl, the pretty Fräulein, or more the city of West Berlin that is being sung about. The lovers meet in spring, the trees are in bloom, it is warm and they stroll through the city in love. They take the S-Bahn to Wannsee, stroll back across Ku-Damm and go home. Every man for himself? That remains to be seen. They met at the radio tower, kissed in love at Wannsee, stood holding hands at the zoo and found it hard to say goodbye to each other. Forever? The song says: "I only have you in mind and my Berlin".

Musically, the love story is embedded in the blues/pop genre, small orchestra with trumpet, played as a fanfare, chanson/schlager style. "Das ist die Berliner Luft" is heard first, then the melody of the song is played by an organ grinder. The performer is the still young Chis Howland. With his English accent, he performs the song very successfully. "Little Girl from Berlin" entered the charts at the beginning of 1960 and remained there for eight weeks.

My Fraulein

Part of the understanding of the song is the situation in West-Berlin and the Allies stationed there. Life was already good again in West-Berlin, reconstruction was in full swing, the Kurfürstendamm was the showcase of the West, at least for the people in East Berlin, now the capital of the GDR. A little later, the Wall came down and Berlin was now a truly divided city.

In the western part, the Berlin Brigade of the Americans, the British at the Reichssportfeld and the French in the Napoleon Quarter had made themselves at home. The soldiers transferred to Berlin did not stay permanently, mostly those from overseas had a girlfriend here, then went back to their families or took the girlfriend home with them as their wife. In the song, the memory of the happy time in Berlin remains. The performer Chris Howland was deployed with the BFN (British Forces Network). He spent his retirement with his fourth wife Monika in Rösrath near Cologne, not in Berlin.

The song reminds me a lot of my own time back then. In love, engaged, married, to whom? To a girl called Monika. We had a small apartment not far from the Ku-Damm. It wasn't far to stroll there and we often took the boat out on the Wannsee. It was a happy time. No wonder you don't get sentimental when you hear this song. There is also a farewell to the young woman, to Berlin. With the song in my head, I still visit both her, the long remarried woman, and my Berlin, even though I live on the Rhine.

What does the song mean to the listener today? A beautiful hit from back then, romantic, perhaps even kitschy. After all, it's a love song. It's meant to evoke  memories of love in spring, and memories of a special city. Not a beautiful one, but a great one, a city that was destroyed, occupied, divided and rebuilt. A place of longing after all. Love in spring in a flourishing city.

I only have you and my Berlin in mind

Experiences on the water

From a red rubber dinghy to a mega cruise ship

The pleasures on the water began quite harmlessly. After all, Berlin has one of the most beautiful bodies of water right under your nose. A rubber dinghy, especially a second-hand one, doesn't cost the earth and if you don't want to paddle, you'll have to make do with an outboard motor. That's a start. What more could you want - yes! As they say, always a hand's breadth of water under the keel. So we had to get a keel, complete with dinghy. One for more than two tails, with a solid bottom and windshield. Purely as an indication, the 3 hp engine produced more of a gentle breeze.

You can't keep up with the sailors, you always have to dodge them and somehow you end up taking the sportier option. So then a sailing boat, without a keel, but with a centerboard, without an engine, a dinghy. But you have to learn to sail, get a berth and, if you want to travel with it, a boat trailer with a hitch and registration. That's a whole different ball game. And the best thing is that pleasure craft with engines have to take evasive action. What about encounters with motorboats? Every sports boat school can provide information.

Sailing as a water sport eclipses any group dynamic process. Sailing courses and experiences with unfamiliar watercraft under sail leave plenty of room to participate in the process. What is the alternative: sailboarding, officially for windsurfing, or stand-up paddling? The dynamic process is best carried out with the elements of air and water. More with one, less with the other. The good thing is that you stay in tune with the trend, and some even stay a little longer.

If you want to get into mischief on the waterways, charter a cabin cruiser. Commercial skippers and insurance companies are grateful for anyone who has a pleasure craft license. At sea, there is also the sea rescue service. I always donate diligently to the DLRG. Nevertheless, you can still make beautiful river trips. The very brave (with a license) can sail past the Chancellery or down the ship's elevator to the Oder and then through the old locks from the time of the Old Fritz. With larger boats, the group dynamic process sets in again, especially when handling them.

In later years, you become a mutant, from self-steering to passenger. Then river cruises are the order of the day. It's manageable and the shore isn't that far away. Others disappear straight into the amusement park on mega cruise ships.

Experiences on the water

Traveling along a river can be quite sporty. The skipper is delighted when all the cyclists have disembarked and are back on board after 30 km. The same applies to those who are eager to learn. Only some lazybones enjoy life on board, culture yes, but then please take the bus. At the cultural events on board, you almost become a local.

Let's move on to the musical steamers (Musikdampfern), as they used to be called. They have not been powered by steam for a long time now, but by huge 2-stroke diesel engines or gas turbines converted to electric propulsion. The clouds of steam, i.e. the exhaust fumes, have remained. But things are changing. Today, going on a long voyage is a mass pleasure. Without any understanding of culture, let alone language, people are wandering around the world. Only the Americans are smarter, they stay on board in their small floating towns and enjoy themselves. Thank goodness there is a wide range on offer, from exclusive yacht life to the hustle and bustle on the cheap boats.

Experiences on the water are so varied, let's dive in. Oh no, then we're in the water!

From the red rubber dinghy

The waters of West Berlin are some of the most beautiful in the country, from the Oberhavel to Potsdam. And who wouldn't want to sail on them?

Everyone starts small, including me. With an Inka S from Metzeler, a red rubber dinghy. I bought it second-hand with a 3 hp Johnson outboard. Quality 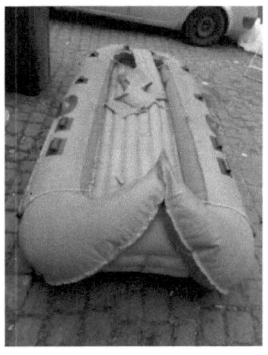 goods, not something from Aldi or Lidl. That was in the mid-60´s of the last century.

And Monika and I used to chug around on the Havel. The Lower Havel area, mostly from Lieper Bay. It was easy to reach by car via the Havelchaussee. Unpack the boat, inflate it (with an air pump), put the outboard on, put gas in the tank, put in some provisions (most beers) and Heidewitzka. Don't forget the safety bolt for the propeller. My comments on a Good Friday trip are very informative. Attached.

The inflatable boat was more of a bathing boat, not really suitable for a long trip. That's why we had to get a bigger one. But more about that later. I sold the boat to Peter Kauschke, without an engine. He had bought a very cheap doldrums pusher. And that came in handy later on.

I want to tell you the story now:

Peter took the rubber boat with him on vacation to Villa Marina de Cesinatico. We both went out and played combat swimmer. At full speed, one of us went overboard, did a lap and picked up again. As we lacked the necessary coordination, we went overboard and the boat headed for Yugoslavia. We had no choice but to look after him and swim ashore, thankfully with flippers, but for a very long time. Thanks to the lousy engine and the current, the boat also went ashore. I spotted it in a crowd of people further down the beach. Everyone was happy that the boat was mine. So, still a little excited, I chugged back to our beach at Bagno Ines. And then we had a good cappuccino and some decent grappa.

Villa Marina Cesenatico Bagno Ines, today

Experiences on the water

Always a hand's breadth of water under the keel

This pious wish of sailors can only be fulfilled if you have a boat with a keel. And such a boat was needed. It was made of rubber, had a solid keel (insert), a solid bottom, a windshield and was suitable for at least four people. An inflatable boat from Wiking, new for a mere DM 1,000. It actually needed a larger outboard motor, but on the Havel more than 3 hp required a license.

Now it was more comfortable on the Havel. At weekends with Monika and occasionally with my friends from the Berlin College. Mostly on the Lower Havel. Heidewitzka!

Just getting the boat ready was more work. At least we already had an electric air pump.

Now there are friends of water sports who want to enjoy its pleasures but don't know the simplest commands. And that's what happened:

I once went out with Peter Kausche and some other landlubbers. We also had Peter's cheap motor screwed on or in tow on the red rubber boat. An American patrol boat overtook us in the Kleiner Wannsee. To avoid the waves, I asked the people sitting opposite to lift up. And what did they do, they stood up and Peter and I fell overboard. Soaking wet, we climbed back into the boat and turned back. Full speed ahead with two engines on the transom. We landed an hour later, soaked and frozen through. We packed up the boat in a hurry and got into the bathtub. I can still see us in front of me, Peter and I on the edge of the bathtub. Monika was glad she hadn't been there.

In that case, less water under the keel would have done the trick.

Experiences on the water

At this point we went overboard

***

The well-traveled dinghy

What is a dinghy? It is a boat without a keel, but with a centerboard, with standing and running rigging, with halyards and sheets. And with a main and a jib. But more about that later.

After chugging around with the engine* (it now had to be sailing under sail* (*termini according to sport boat license). So I sold the Viking and Johnson and bought a 420 dinghy (used with standing rigging: wooden mast and main boom). This is the little sister of the 470 racing dinghy, which is still an Olympic boat class today. For sailing freaks, there's also the 505, with a trapeze and a really large sail area. I had to ferry the dinghy from Gatow to the Pichelsee-Havelschenke, Bootshaus Keser. This is by the Freibrücke bridge, a little further than the well-known TU sailing club boathouse. I had rigged the dinghy and wanted to set off, but unfortunately my sailing skills were rather theoretical. I was glad that I had Peter's lousy outboard with me. Besides, the 420 is a 2-man boat. During my studies, I was out on the water with Joachim Gebhardt almost every Sunday during the season.

Now Joachim came up with the idea that we could sail somewhere else, the Mediterranean would be good. A boat trailer was needed, a trailer coupling had to be screwed on and the whole thing had to be approved by TÜV. OK, it worked. Only if it hadn't been for the towing vehicle, a Citroen

Diane with 18 hp. A bit weak on the chest. Actually, we only wanted to go to the Camargue coast, but the waves were too high there. So we continued via the

Pyrenees to the Costa Brava. And we did, very slowly up the mountains. We also sailed, with a rental dinghy. We sailed back via Lac d'Annesy in Savoy, where we really sailed with the 420s. Yes - that's how you get to know the world on the water.

The next time we were to go to my friends' vacation paradise, Villa Mariana de Cesenatico. With a more powerful engine, a VW Beetle with 44 hp. Volker Q. was the co-pilot. And he had to prove himself on the water, with two other sailing experts. I shouldn't have given them the boat, because there are sailing

schools for a reason. It came as it had to: the shroud on the port bow had lost its attachment (shackle), the mast was in danger of tipping over, and it could have been reattached with a piece of the running rigging. But only if you knew how to use the sheet. It is still a mystery to me how they managed to get the boat back without damaging the "keelson" (please look it up). And now the lazybones are lying there as if nothing had happened.

Once again, the dinghy went on vacation to Denmark with Gunhild. Sonderburg on the Flensburg Fjord. We had rented a vacation apartment there and found a berth for the boat. It was a wonderful vacation, as the pictures show.

I sold the boat to Claus Sch. He could have used a sailing course at the TU. I felt a bit sorry for the "Wanderjolle".

Sailing with Gottfried Möller

It's not just Berlin's waters that are the most beautiful, there are also some on Mallorca. Not just Ballermann, the bay of Porto Pollensa, for example, in the very east of the island. This is where Gottfried Möller has been running his sailing school Sail&Surf for more than 40 years. More about that in a moment.

Now permanently employed as a non-boat owner in faraway Wessiland, a good ten years before reunification, I didn't want to miss out on life on the water. There was a great offer from Gottfried to get to know me: flight, accommodation in a double room, half board, sailing course, all for a small DM. So "up sea" again. And find out which boat is the most fun. Under sail, I mean.

It started harmlessly enough. Sailing theory, knot tying, casting off and mooring, sea maneuvers, etc. Everything I had already learned on the

Experiences on the water

TU sailing course. Then we sailed in the Galeon dinghy regatta (here's the photo of the finish: Porto Pollensa 29.09.1979). I was the skipper and we should have won. Yes, if the crew hadn't got in line. You know how it is!

Then I felt like something bigger, like a keelboat. So I went out on a keel cruiser. The skipper either had no idea and/or was very seaworthy. Always against the swell in the bay of Alcudia. I was completely exhausted when the conviction in the cabin got to me. I've never felt so sick in my life. The fish got plenty of food. Since then I've known that taking a sailing yacht out to sea is not for me.

Here is a small gallery from the sailing school, with a recommendation to pay Gottfried a visit. Maybe he'll be at the boat show in Düsseldorf again. I visited him twice more, once with Gunhild and once with my daughter Solveig for her 10th birthday. More about that another time.

Experiences on the water

Windsurfing or stand-up paddleboarding?

Now we are at the trend sports on the water. The current one from 40 years ago was windsurfing, called sailing surfing on the license. It's for dynamic people like my brother-in-law Bruno, family have to be able to keep your balance. Can I still do that?

Let's talk about back then. Being boatless and traveling for water under the keel was nothing either. And who doesn't like to be trendy? So I bought a windsurfing board, not one of the popular Mistral boards, but with a sail area of 5.7 square meters and a displacement of 210 liters. Don't forget the roof rack.

The next thing I did was to take a windsurfing course with a work colleague on a fishing pond in Hesse. I don't remember whether the windsurfing license was compulsory.

I once took my brother-in-law to Lake Otto Maigler and he didn't want to get off the boat, or rather off the board. That was and is something for him. Windsurfing in the Aegean, that's it, and for the whole family.

I didn't go there, but I did go to the Mediterranean, as always to Villa Marina de Cesenatico. I gave the "Amarillo buoy" there, which means: I stood in the water and those who wanted to, surfed around me at my command. I was wearing a red cap and not a yellow one. Our friend Werner S. already has a racing surfboard and has sailed far out. He's always been a madman.

And, believe it or not, a certain Mrs. Eleonore, which is my wife, got her windsurfing license from Tonio in Villa Marina. Congratulations!

I later sold the board to my fencing buddy Dieter D. from Mainz, it was just right for his 110 kg. I never stood on a surfboard again after that, maybe I should try stand-up paddling.

Sailing with Gottfried Möller again

For Solveig's 10th birthday, I gave her a sailing course as a present. And where should it be? With Gottfried Möller on Mallorca, of course. So I booked the flight, rental car, apartment and course. For me, the only option was something faster. Try out the 470 racing dinghy or the Hobbycat catamaran. To anticipate, I capsized with both. But more about that later. Solveig's efforts at sailing were sincere, but without success. She also preferred to sit at Gottfried's sailing bar with a sweet drink. She got a certificate anyway. Here's the sweetheart, chic, isn't it.

Gottfried had more confidence in me. I was allowed on the catamaran as jib monkey, a Hobbycat 16 or 19. The skipper was good, I learned a lot from him.

He even let me use the tiller once. We never capsized either. For those in the know, on a catamaran you tack by jibing.

We were a good crew, but unfortunately he had to go home three days later and I drove him to the airport. Then I was the skipper, an inexperienced jib monkey. And we were already in it, in a high arc. Now the catamaran has a so-called capsize sheet. The boat lies with its sails on the water and you have to put the sheet over the float and pull it (correctly "pullen"). With a bit of luck, the boat will

over to the other side or the boat takes off without a crew. We had both. But Gottfried was careful. He was always in sight. As you can see here.

It was easy to understand that I had had enough of hobby cat sailing. Then it was better to go for the 470 racing dinghy, I knew my way around. Unfortunately, I had another wretch of a bowman, little or no idea. And it came as it had to, a full capsize (keel up, masthead stuck in the bottom), in the harbour

entrance of Porto Pollensa of all places. I had seen it coming and was still sitting on the hull with dry feet. So I put the boat to one side, see picture. The foresailor did this in the water by pulling the centerboard towards the water. I climbed over the side of the boat and secured it so that it didn't flip over to the other side. It worked wonderfully. Gottfried was full of praise. Nothing was broken either.

Experiences on the water

Yes - that was a special experience, especially in the water. Solveig and I are full of experiences. How often I walked to the landing stage.

From pleasure craft with a propulsion engine under ten meters in length

That's what it says in the recreational craft license. In the past, you could use it to drive watercraft up to 22 meters in length, today it is probably up to 15 meters. You don't need one if you have less than 5 hp propulsion power and in certain areas. Whether you charter a boat or call it your own, you must have such a license. This avoids incorrect mooring and casting off, locks and obeying right of way regulations to the amusement or annoyance of others.

I had chartered a motor cruiser a few times, by the way, only landlubbers say rented. These were boats from 6.80 to 10.50 in length. Buying one was one of those thoughts. Where is the boat, how expensive are the running costs and who is willing to come along? Not an option.

Figuratively speaking, I stayed in the regional league. In other words, I sailed around on rivers. I would describe coastal shipping as the top league, but you need a sea license and a certain level of seaworthiness or lots of pills to combat seasickness.

In 1976, Gunhild and I went on a tour of Ireland on the Shennon. Here is a picture from the corresponding report. As you can see, the boat had a nice free steering position (with Gunhild behind it), inside a pentry, usually called a small galley or sideboard on yachts, toilet and cozy bunks in the foredeck. These sports boats are actually easy to handle, but not for everyone. We had moored in front of a pub and I watched together with a seasoned Irishman, who had already had a few pints, as boat charterers moored or wanted to. They fell into the water while mooring because they were pushing the boat away from the shore. What a laugh we had.

In September 2005, we, an elderly couple, went on a city trip by boat. Potsdam and the surrounding area, Berlin waters to the Chancellery. They had chartered a Voyager 780 cabin cruiser from Bootscharter Caputh. First they headed towards Brandenburg an der Havel, past the cherry blossom town of Werder to Paretz. Queen Luise of Prussia spent the best time of her life there in the summer palace with her husband Friedrich Wilhelm III.

You should know that the parking facilities for pleasure craft are signposted accordingly, and it is also worth looking out for the yellow wave. Just by the way.

Now back to the familiar territory, but not before visiting the ferry house restaurant in Caputh.

Onwards across the Spree into the capital. After the Charlottenburg lock, we moored for the night on the Charlottenburg bank. Passers-by found this unusual. Another nice beer in the brewery around the corner, known from the Charlottenburg Christmas market.

Experiences on the water

Sightseeing was the order of the day the next day. There is a mooring possibility in front of the museum island. A larger boat took us alongside. The owners had sold their house and bought a motor yacht, gypsies (used as a synonym) on the water. Back across the Charlottenburg lock, a disaster on the way down, the lock keeper's cheeks were puffed out. Yes - locks need to be learned. We, the older couple, were lucky. We were able to moor up at a sailing club on Stößensee and stay overnight. They were having a party and "we're in". A donation for the club's coffers.

At the end of the tour, we invited Hans and Annette C. to take us on a tour of Potsdam and around the Pfaueninsel. Peter and Renate Kauschke didn't want to go. At the end of the tour, we went to the Fährhausrestaurant Caputh. The elderly couple still remember the wonderful water experience today.

Havel island Werder with mill and church

Experiences on the water

From sports boats with a propulsion engine over ten meters long

If you want to take several water sports enthusiasts with you, you need long boats and even longer patience. I want to tell you about both.

In September 2007, the elderly couple were on a boat trip in Brandenburg with Heide and Volkmar K.. They had met the aforementioned couple on an Indian summer cruise. This time they all wanted to experience something on their own boat, i.e. a motor yacht. We had chartered a 10.5 m boat, the "Viktoria". She had everything we needed: Fore and aft cabin, pentry, toilet and, above all, a flying bridge. A flying bridge is an outside steering position, usually with a lounge and retractable top, from which you have a good view of the waterway. And on top a bow thruster rudder, a great thing for maneuvering.

We set off from the old harbor of the Zehdenick brick factory on the Havel. As early as 1901, electrically powered Finow barges were used to transport bricks from there to Berlin. Interesting, isn't it? You reach the Oder-Havel Canal via the Liebenwalde lock. The lock was the first challenge for the crew and the skipper's nerves. Navigating the canal with pleasure craft is a tricky business. The large cargo ships, mostly Polish, have a considerable pull. We were glad to be able to enter a small marina beforehand.

The next day to the Niederfinow boat lift (Schiffshebewerk Niederfinow), a highlight of our boat tour. Embarked and 36 m down, the pictures say more. Shortly before reaching the Oder in Hohenwutzen harbor, we had another delicious dinner in a restaurant. The skipper had to recover, the crew had a look at the surroundings.

Then it was back along the old Finow Canal, passing through ten historic locks. Most of the locks are from the time of the Old Fritzen.

Much to the delight of the skipper and the lock keepers, the crew had now mastered the locks perfectly. And don't forget to tip ten times.

Back on the Oder-Havel waterway, we made our way to Werbelinsee. Friendly people helped to moor the boat, the harbour master held out his hand. The skipper took care of the mess and the crew went to eat smoked fish. Lake Werbelin is located in the middle of the Schorfheide. It has been populated by the more and less illustrious. Theodor Fontane, Hermann Göring, Erich Honecker and his "friend" Helmut Schmidt, in turn.

Back to Zehdenick again. The boat remained intact, nothing happened, although we were close. Farewell dinner in the restaurant at the old harbor. We spent the night on the boat one last time. One last visit to the historic brickworks park, then it was off home.

***

Experiences on the water

Just this year, our fencing friend Wolfram K. came up with the idea that the senior fencers could go on a boat trip on the waterways of our Dutch neighbors. He knew his way around there, but hadn't yet been on a big boat. The Waterkaart Friesland shows Sneek as the starting point, with a motorboat 11 meters long. It must have been a barge before. We had planned to make the waterways around Sneek

unsafe. Wolfram was the skipper, I was his co-skipper and we were joined by the fencers Helmuth K., Elmar St., Dr. Frank E. and "Klausi" (last name forgotten). It was very busy, especially on the Sneeker Meer.

The long ship was quite a challenge, especially in the small canals. It also didn't have a flying bridge, but a steering position in the middle. Well - an almost historic boat. The visit to Leeuwarden was nice. Sailing into a big city, having a chic meal and playing Doppelkopf with accessories (Olde Genever) in the cabin in the

evening. And another experience, there can only be one skipper. The following pictures show the crew at breakfast and in a moored position in Leeuwarden.

Whether around Berlin, de Paris Nord or the Duoro Valley...

What does the water sports enthusiast do in old age? Mutate into a passenger! But even that can be done in different ways. Let's take a look at the river cruise.

Experiences on the water

Not the one from Passau down the Danube, but an active, a cultural and an adventure-oriented river cruise, each and together.

The active version of the river cruise is called Boat & Bike. You usually whizz along the river on a bike and return to your bunk, or cabin, in the evening. We, the youngest daughter by far, took a cruise around Berlin, from Spandau to

Potsdam, cycled through Sanssouci, across the Teltow Canal to Köpenick, cycled to Prenzlauer Berg, to the Berlin Wall, spent the night in front of the Palace of Tears and back to Spandau near Berlin.

Our boat was the Marylou, a converted barge with a crew of three. There were 16 guests on board and the atmosphere was informal. I have fond memories of the pleasant evening with the crew over a small beer.

Let's move on to the culture cruise. The A-Rosa shipping company had offered a bargain cruise that we couldn't say no to. The train journey on the Tallis train was almost as expensive. The A-Rosa Viva, a 130-metre-long riverboat, was to set off from Saint Denis in the north of Paris. Unfortunately, it was high tide, so we boarded the bus at this point. What felt like hours later, we finally boarded the ship through the evening traffic. Down the Seine to the highlights of Normandy, the city of Rouen and the castle of Richard the Lionheart, Chateau Gaillard. The food on the ship was "first class", the cabin unusually large and nicely furnished for a river ship. A recommendation.

Experiences on the water

There was a lot going on culturally: Rouen with the Old Market, where Jean d'Arc was burned, the heart of Richard the Lionheart in the cathedral, the plague courtyard, the clock tower with the Gros Horloge. And don't forget an original Calvados. The Chateau Gaillard was another matter, difficult to climb. Once at the top, you learn the history of the castle. Creepy. The view of the river is all the more beautiful. A walk to the small town of Les Andelys is also worthwhile. Back in Paris, we went to Montmartre and for Sunday lunch, not without culture either, to a nice family restaurant nearby

In the fall of 2019, the older couple, i.e. us, hungry for adventure as we were, took a trip down the valley. Actually, there were two. We took the Teleférico de Gaia (a cable car from the Duoro bridge down to the river) to the landing stage where the nikco cruise boat was waiting for us. This took us to the UNESCO World Heritage Douro Valley. I can't tell you about everything we experienced on the trip. So I'll just give one example.

Experiences on the water

The Carrapatelo lock is one of the largest (or deepest) of the five on the Douro River. With a 35 m stroke, the process takes about 12 minutes. Everything on the sun deck is laid down for the passage. Passengers must remain seated for the next bridge. Some people have already slipped off their chairs, it was that close. In the lock, it's like being in a deep hole.

On the way, we visited castles, vineyards and very old villages. Finally, a detour to Salamanca, one of the most beautiful cities in Spain. The food on board was typically good, there was

nothing to complain about in the cabin and the company at the table was very pleasant.

The widespread opinion that river cruises are only for gruffies, in German old people, in English the grumpy ones, is simply not true. Even

if you are a mutant.

Experiences on the water

Auf großer Fahrt **you need a** **ship master´s certificates**

The difference between "grand voyage" and "great voyage" can be explained as follows: *„Auf großer Fahrt"* is a patent or certificate of competency for someone, usually a captain (patent A5, a sample, not mine), who is responsible for hundreds of employees and thousands of passengers at sea. On a great voyage, sometimes even during the voyage, there are people who expose themselves to the responsibility for others for more or less money, i.e. take a cruise.

Much has been written about the growing cruise craze, from environmentalists and historians to cruise fans. As a notorious cruise fan, I have had the following experiences over the years.

Our first cruise - the older couple were still working full time - was more of a transit cruise, across the Atlantic to Indian Summer in New England, USA. The Jewel of the Seas was a brand-new megaship from Royal Caribbian International, almost 300 meters long, for 2,112 people without responsibility

(for the ship), 46 km/h fast. A real music steamer, as the sailors used to say. The whole thing was a group trip for

academics. With the old days of cruising in mind, we had dressed up accordingly, i.e. tailor-made dress, dinner jacket, tux. We needed them for posing with the captain. The evenings in formal attire were great: festive dinners, Broadway shows, hanging out in the bar with Bombay Sapphyré gin.

Experiences on the water

We remained friends with the K. couple traveling with us for years to come.

In between, we crossed the pond several more times, with ships sometimes faster (Vision of the Seas), sometimes larger (Freedom of the Seas). But now on our own and always in connection with longer shore leave (Florida, Alaska, Argentina and many more). That way you get to know other people, you don't

always want to meet your own countrymen. We actually used the ship as a comfortable means of transportation. Just as the German shipowners envisioned it in the 1930s, with scheduled services to the New World. This is still the case today with the Queen May II operated by Cunard Line.

We have stayed with the U.S. shipping company. We have had good experiences and have been busy collecting cruise points. There's something about going to the Diamond Lounge, eating delicious canapés and filling up on excellent drinks. The last cruise was in the 5-star segment of RCCL, a ship from Celebrity Cruise Line, the "Millennium", not a very large but elegant ship. We don't need all-round

entertainment on board, organized early-morning exercise for Mrs. Eleonore does the trick too. Listen to the lectures, take part in a cooking or language course, enjoy a convivial meal and then watch the theater show.

Experiences on the water

We are not following the trend. There are a number of club ships that have everything on board. The American ones with a half to full amusement park on board, the German ones with a private brewery and relaxed behavior patterns. Preferably all inclusive.

This is how we say goodbye, like here to Singapore. Not without planning our next experiences on the water.

Brewery Tours

Northern brewery tour in Kölle*

Dear friends of Kölsch** and hikers,

Here is a short description of my northern brewery tour "From St. Ursula via St. Peter and Marien"

From the main station forecourt, turn left through Dompropst-Ketzer-Straße into Marzellenstraße. Passing the only baroque church in Cologne, you reach the crossing over the north-south drive, where you can already see the church of St. Ursula on the half-left.

The "chamber of horrors" (Schreckenskammer) is already closed early on Friday evening, but the pub of the same name right next door is still open. You also don't have to look into the deep eye sockets of the skulls stacked in the Golden Chamber of St. Ursula. Those who do anyway can recover from their horror in the pub, where even the Kölsch beer has the same name. There are still seats available at this time. I recommend the brisket.

After a few delicious Kölsch beers, head back the way you came to An den Dominikanern. A few meters to the right, then left into an alley where you can see the church. It's worth going inside first for the Gregorian chants sung by the monks between seven and half past seven, and when they're not singing, you can learn something about St. Andrew, the patron saint of the brewers' guild. You can read more in the brewery guide.

At the exit of the church, take the small alley on the left across the large street, then take the small staircase to the castle wall (street), in an easterly direction you will see the High Cathedral of Cologne, St. Peter and St. Mary. Walk up to the café and guess which of the two towers is higher. If you guess correctly, you get a round of Kölsch.

From there, turn half right to Rocalliplatz. The witches' prisons used to be on the corner of the Dom-Hotel. They were later burned on Melaten. To cheer yourself up, head to Früh am Hof. Where the beer barrels in the cellar are elevated. You can still have a good chat there. If a table is free, I recommend a keg, available from 9 liters.

If you haven't looked too deeply into the glass, take a look at the beer mat: It says: "Cölner Hofbräu - Früh". You can understand that "Früh" comes from the company founder Peter Josef Früh, not the "Hofbräu", the glasses are too small for that. Rather, this has to do with Mr. Früh's strong marketing efforts, as the brewery is located "Am Hof", which sounds like something higher.

After a few more delicious Kölsch beers, it's off to the Sion in Untern-Taschenmacher-Straße or the Peters-Brauhaus in Mühlengasse, depending on the size of the barrel and the number of liters of Kölsch "handled". Both can be reached by walking along Am Hofe towards the Rhine and then keeping to the right.

Have fun

* By Kölle, the people of Cologne mean their city "Köln"

** Kölsch is a sort of special beer brewed in Cologne and also the dialect the people sproken

***

Southern brewery tour in Kölle

Dear friends of Kölsch and hikers,

Here is a short description of my southern brewery tour "From Klein St. Martin to Groß St. Martin"

From Neumarkt, take a train on the right bank of the Rhine to Heumarkt. Get on at the back and get off. After a few steps back, you are right next to the Gothic tower of the former parish church of Klein St. Martin. Walking around to the left, you will see the church of St. Maria im Kapitol straight ahead. Then cross the street and take the steps to the right into the "Lichhof", the funeral yard. The mourner in the middle indicates this. Cross the "Leichenhof" to the "Dreikünningepörzje". Walk through once and from Marienplatz back through the gate. Look up to the left and admire the Romanesque building. No longer think of Kaspar, Melchior and Balthasar, but of Jupiter, Juno and Minerva, who used to be worshipped here.

Back through the gate again, then left across the large street into Rheingasse, where you can already see the oldest patrician house in Cologne, the

Overstolzenhaus, on the right. With your back to the house, you can see a small alley with a gateway. We now pretend to want to buy a Pittermännchen (10-liter barrel) in the Malzmühle (brewery). So, through the side entrance directly to Zappes and Thekenschaaf. A great place: you can wait for a seat, watch the professional tapping and the Kölsch will certainly not be long in coming. You can leave the brewery via the revolving door. Outside you can see the Prussians (monument) and, further back, Groß St. Martin.

Through the underpass onto Heumarkt. On the left-hand side, roughly in the middle, you will find a fish sandwich, the snack bar is called "Op d'r Fescheck". Freshly fortified, cross the square into "Markmannsgasse" to the Hänneschen Puppet Theater. Shortly before this, we turn left into Eisenmarkt, where "ons Kölsche Jong" is sitting on a bench. As we are now thirsty again, we head straight across the square to Salzgasse, where the "Sünner im Walfisch" brewery is just to the right. The place is always full, so don't be late. The 5-liter beer towers from which you can tap are great fun.

After a few delicious Kölsch beers, turn left and left again onto "Auf dem Rotenberg". After about 50 m on the right, a few steps down, is the "Rote Funke Platz". In the dark, use the flashlight you have brought with you to read out the oath of the Rote Funke. Preferably non-Rhinelanders should do this, as it increases the fun factor immensely. There is a round of Kölsch for every 10 words read incorrectly, so make a note!

The stress-free walkers now circle Groß St. Martin in an anti-clockwise direction, via Lintgasse, Fischmarkt and Mauritiusgasse. Up the steps - opposite the public toilet - the path leads to the church.

Imagine that this is where St. Martin's Island was located, off the Roman harbour. The harbor silted up. Archbishop Bruno founded the Benedictine monastery of St. Martin. The complex with the crossing tower was built in 1150 AD. All described in detail on the "Schmitzsäule". If you look around, you can see the two Cologne originals in the back corner. Rubbing Tünnes' nose brings good luck.

The "Hüßjer bunt am Altermaat" can be reached via Brigittengässchen and Lintgasse. The Alter Markt was built on the silted-up Roman harbor. Ships were moored where the town hall steps begin.

Brewery Tours

What the houses on Alter Markt once looked like can be seen today in the houses at 20 - 22, on the corner of Lintgasse. The best thing about it is that you

can go inside: to the Gaffel private brewery. You should curb your thirst for beer for a moment and look back at the square. This is where the "Gestech" was carried out and heads were chopped off. Today, people jostle and sway for all they're worth on 11.11. When looking at the Jan van Werth monument, you should also remember the sentence from Griet at the bottom of the monument: "Jo, Jan, wer et hät jewoß" (If I had known that, I would have married you).

But now inside, and don't forget, whoever read out the text the worst at the Rote Funken gets a round.

After a few more delicious Kölsch beers, it's off to the Sion brewery "Untern Taschenmacher" or the Peters brewery in Mühlengasse. Both can be reached in the direction of the cathedral.

Have fun

***

Southern brewery tour to Haus Töller

Dear friends of Kölsch and hikers,

You now know the southern brewery tour "From Klein St. Martin to Groß St. Martin". As we don't want to miss out on the walking, we're adding a second leg, which goes as far as Haus Töller in Weyerstrasse / near Barbarossaplatz.

To make the walk of around three quarters of an hour as entertaining as possible, Ele and I dedicated our New Year's walk entirely to the cause.

So we cheerfully left the Gaffel private brewery and turned half left towards Marsplatz, marched around the old pump and in the direction of the Fastnachtsbrunnen (Carnival Fountain), a short prayer to the past and coming carnival times.

Having had enough of remembrance, we walk past St. Alban and Gürzenich in the direction of the Hard Rock Cafe, which we leave to the left. We walk through the Schildergasse without any consumerism. We take note of the

Brewery Tours

Antoniterkirche church in its architectural form and the possibility of re-entering the church. In 2004 there were over 400 people, if I can believe my superintendent.

We cross under Neumarkt via the escalator and come back into the light of day at the public health department. Now into Thieboldsgasse, past the premises of the Jan van Werth equestrian choir, who must already be rehearsing for carnival. At the Lungengasse junction, we pause and Ele will say something medical.

Now carry on, don't miss Alexianerstraße. So, turn right and continue to the end. On the right is the baroque Palais Wolkenburg, which was decorated for Christmas during our tour. Our destination is not far to the left, opposite a beautiful old schnapps distillery.

We are standing on Weyerstrasse in front of Haus Töller and the reserved seats inside tempt us to sit down, enjoy a cool Kölsch and some delicious food.

I hope it will be a long Sunday evening.

***

Western brewery tour in Kölle

Dear friends of Cologne and hikers,

Here are some directions for the brewery tour "From St. Pantaleon via St. Severin."

You can get to St. Pantaleon's Abbey either through the gateway into the inner courtyard of the old people's home, with a good view of the early Romanesque church in all its grandeur. It is one of the twelve large Romanesque basilicas in Cologne's old town. So, then around the church into the interior, mass is at 6.30

pm and the church is open. Out through the small gate in the direction of "Unter den sieben Burgen"

Shortly before the north-south drive, the baroque complex of the Carmelite nuns "Maria vom Frieden" is illuminated.

We then reach the area of the Charterhouse "House of the Protestant Church, baroque 3-winged complex, next to it the Carthusian Church, Lady Chapel in the

side aisle, ask the sexton. Behind the church is a beautiful inner courtyard (cloister of the former monastery).

Visit the Wirtz restaurant around the corner. Keep left in the direction of Severinsstraße. It's supposed to be quaint, a typical Cologne neighborhood pub. Then cross Severinsstraße in the direction of the traditional Schmitze-Lang pub and continue to Severinstorburg and Chlodwigplatz. We stop off at the pub with its distillery and distillery bar and strange name. At http://de.pluspedia.org/wiki/Schmitze-Lang# we find an explanation: Josef Schmitz, who was a member of the guard regiment in Berlin in the days of the Kaiser. As there were two Schmitzs at the same time and Josef Schmitz was the taller one with a guard height of 204 cm, he was nicknamed "Schmitze-Lang".

But now to a real brewery, the Früh "em Veedel", known as Veedel-Früh. It is located just to the left behind the Torburg castle on Chlodwigplatz. Here's a review from TripAdvisor: "Despite the restaurant being full, the service was friendly and quick, the roast goose was fairly priced at € 29 (geese are very expensive everywhere this year!) and extremely tasty: tender meat, good sauce, fine side dishes. There's no need to praise the good Früh-Kölsch... or the beautiful restaurant with its patina and atmosphere."

Have fun

***

In and near Berlin

The IGA is a garden exhibition and it depends a bit on the season

The International Garden Exhibition Berlin 2017 was created on a park-like site in the Berlin districts of Marzahn and Hellersdorf. Formerly the most notorious planned housing estate in the GDR with a social focus after reunification. Today, the Kienberg offers a central view of the promised landscapes. A cable car connects the Kienbergpark with the Wuhletal. This also justifies the hefty entrance fee of €20. The Gardens of the World are on display. Very nice to walk through. And if you want to hike, you can do this, it feels like 5 km, but is actually only 1,500 m long. One stop is the Wolkenhain on the Kienberg, with wonderful views and a summer toboggan run (for young and old). You should consider when the best flowering time is. The best way to get there is to take the U5 from Alexanderplatz (Kienberg - Gärten der Welt station). It is inconvenient by car, parking lot and shuttle bus.

A good starting point for visitors to Berlin and nothing else is missing

The hotel can be given four stars with a clear conscience. The rooms are located around a courtyard that runs parallel to Chausseestraße. We had a room in the back building, so to speak, very quiet. There's nothing wrong with the breakfast and the service.

In and near Berlin

The Berliner Ballhaus (with Schwof = dancing) is opposite for a beer. Around the corner is the Natural History Museum (which is also the name of the subway station), which is great for children. The nearby Invalidenfriedhof, perhaps not for children, but historically interesting. Watch out, cyclists ride on it. Most of Berlin's sights are within easy reach. If you want to eat something typical, order Eisbein (boiled pork knuckle) with sauerkraut

and mashed peas. The dish consists of more than 1 kg of meat on the bone, so don't be ashamed to order a second plate for your partner. For this meal, go to Mutter Hoppe or the Gerichtslaube, both in the Nikolai quarter. Enjoy your meal.

"For my lame soldiers ..." Frederick II.

Old Fritz had the Invalids' House built and the Invalids' Cemetery laid out next to it. There they lay, the "lame" soldiers, mostly generals and above. But there were also civilians, who also had to be buried. So a part was left to the local community. Then came the division of Germany and, unfortunately, the cemetery was located on the border. You can still see this today on the cycle path that runs through it, formerly the border strip. Be careful not to stand on it, the cyclists are coming fast. Apart from a few restored graves, there is not much left to see.

Nevertheless, a quiet place in the center of Berlin. The history of the cemetery can be read on two plaques. But only in German.

On Museum Island there is an information box for the new building of the Berlin City Palace, the Humboldt Forum

If you have had enough of the many museums, take a look at the large new building opposite. An info box has been set up for this purpose, just across the street from the silver building. No entrance fee, but a restaurant on the 5th floor and toilets everywhere. On the 5th floor there are 2 balconies, on one you can watch the hard-working construction workers, on the other you have a view of the Forum Fridericianum (to the west) and to the east you can see the television tower and Alexanderplatz behind it. Straight ahead is the Altes Museum and a little to the right is Berlin Cathedral. In the lower rooms

you can admire a model of the Berlin City Palace. And of course what the Humboldt Forum will look like later (very good animation). So it's really worth going inside.

A quick trip to the toilet and then around the Humboldt Forum

You're standing in front of the Lustgarten with the Altes Museum and suddenly there's a must. Well - then hurry into the Humboldt Box, there's one in the exhibition and one in the restaurant. Afterwards there are several alternatives: on the terrace with a beer and a view of the Linden and Alexanderplatz, the exhibition or a tour around the Humboldt Forum construction site. We did the latter, but to the left. Crossing the Schlossfreiheit and the bridge of the same name takes you to Schinkelplatz with the Feak Building Academy behind it. From there you can already see the dimensions of the Forum with its dome.

Continue around to the south side. You can already see the ornamentation through the scaffolding. Then you cross the lock bridge, where the weirs of the Kupfergraben rush by. And then to the Spree, over which the new

Rathausbrücke bridge crosses. Very successful with the back of the Forum. We recommend a stop at Julchen Hoppe, an old Berlin restaurant. Maybe just a Berliner Weisse or a pork knuckle with sauerkraut and mashed potatoes. Strengthened or not, it's off through the park, Marx and Engels send their regards. The yellow containers meandering through the park advertise the new U5 subway line. It will run from Alexanderplatz to the Brandenburg Gate and beyond. That's why the boulevard Unter den Linden is a huge construction site. Finally, we return to our starting point, the Humboldt Box.

Finally a view of the almost finished palace on the open construction site day

In previous years, we used to sneak around the huge construction site of the palace / Humboldt Forum. There was already a palace before that, probably a socialist one, then for many years the Christmas hype, the palace fake, and now the building site. On Sunday, August 26, we and many others were allowed inside. Thank God we arrived very early, by midday the crowd was almost at Alexanderplatz. We listened to what Mr. von Boddien had to say in the Schlüterhof, walked around the 2nd floor and then listened to the concert by the Berlin State and Cathedral Choir.

Comfortable in the donation café. The mother next to us had two boys in the boys' choir. We can only say that the palace/forum is really great and we are looking forward to when everything is finished. We'll be there, as the people of Cologne say during carnival.

In and near Berlin

From Potsdamer Platz to the Brandenburg Gate

This time I wanted to find out how far Potsdamer Platz had been rebuilt. I took the route to the Brandenburg Gate. There are also smaller things that distract from the magnificent buildings. Not everyone notices that the first traffic lights in Germany are switched in exactly the same way as modern traffic lights all around, only the lights change horizontally instead of vertically. The remains of the wall opposite are also quite vivid. And well commented. Further towards Tiergarten, the crowned "capital city bear" stands in front of the Marriott.

Simply cute. Diagonally opposite you can see the parade of the "United Buddy Bears" and, if you look closely, the green traffic light man in large. Past the memorial to the Jewish victims, you can already see the Brandenburg Gate, surrounded by tourists. If you want to continue, take the bus in the direction of the television tower and see how far the construction of the Humboldt Forum has progressed.

In and near Berlin

From the pleasureground to the fountain

Part of Babelsberg Palace Park and the palace have been exquisitely restored, especially the pleasureground, the fountains and the fountain. Almost as Prince Pückler would have imagined it. The view of the river Havel with the bridge and across to Potsdam is unique - as is the view of the palace across the lines of sight. Prussian Arcadia!

The approach from Berlin is via the narrow bridge over the Teltow Canal. There are few parking spaces just behind it. It's better to drive up the hill and into the castle park entrance. Despite the parking ban, people park here collectively. There is a self-service restaurant in front of the bridge, Augustiner Hell beer. Or you can go to the ice cream parlor on the other side of the street. We really enjoyed the outing with our loved ones.

In and near Berlin

Now you can also visit Babalsberg Castle - the Prince Pückler exhibition

Even if it's difficult to get there and the parking spaces are few and far between, it's especially worth it now. You can enter the castle for the Fürst Pückler exhibition. The entrance fee is €10 and you are given an admission time. We had 50 minutes. So we made a mini-excursion to the Flatow Tower and only made it as far as the Old Courthouse. This dates from 1270 and was a gift from

the citizens of Berlin to Kaiser Wilhelm II when the old town hall was demolished and the new (red) one was built. The delinquents were chained in the Gothic arches. Today you can see through them to the Flatow Tower.

The life of Prince Pückler is exhibited in documents and pictures in four rooms. Very informative. If you want more Pückler, you have to go to Branitz or Muskau. We strolled back to the parking lot, crossing the Teltow Canal by car to reach an outdoor restaurant. Please note: get your drinks first, then your food and then pay, otherwise the food will be cold.

In and near Berlin

Before Christmas in Berlin

It wasn't the first time we had visited Berlin before Christmas. But this time we had big plans, especially as we couldn't resist the special offers from the train and hotel.

We traveled 1st class all the way to Berlin, without a stopover, in four hours. Deutsche Bahn calls this sprinting. At the Maritim Hotel in Freidrichstraße, it wasn't the same with class: none of the single beds we had ordered, king-size instead, shower in the bathtub. All good - we didn't complain. We didn't have much time to relax as we had to pay the obligatory visit to Hans and Annette. We took the S1 to Zehlendorf, then the bus - I always forget which one - and walked 400 meters to Brandenburg. Beautiful Christmas tree, wonderful chat. It was getting late. We were driven to the bus.

10 o'clock the next morning, time slot open for the Neue Nationalgalerie. All the paintings by important 20th century painters are on display. Excavation work is going on next door so that more pictures can be hung up soon. Then we'll be back. Next door, the lights were on in St. Matthew's Church, so it was time to take a look inside. A friendly man explained the building to us and invited us to come back the next day, there would be a reading with organ music at lunchtime. We decided to do it. Traditionally, we stopped off at "Mutter Hoppe"

on the Fischerinsel. This time, no pork knuckle with pea puree, but a giant cabbage roulade and fried goose liver with mashed potatoes. Before that, we had inspected the new stations on the subway line 5. We liked the "Museum Island" station with its starry sky the best. Tea at Monika and Georg's. Another beautiful Christmas tree, decorated just like in the days of the emperor. Which brings us to the topic: We discussed Georg's new book about the German Empire's Orient policy. Interesting in connection with the jihad. And we paid tribute to Monika's efforts on the piano. It will be some time before Beethoven gets his turn.

After the visit, the Christmas market on Breitscheitplatz offered itself, past the beautifully decorated shop windows of KADEWE. The reason was the search for a special tree decoration, the curved red and white candy canes. We found them at the special stall. We had another Berlin currywurst with spicy onions and a few potato pancakes. That was a nice day.

Another 10 a.m., this time it was the Humboldt Forum's turn. Even without a time slot, it was possible to visit the "Berlin Global" exhibition. It showed the history of Berlin in the world. Interesting and worth knowing. At 12 o'clock we took the new subway to Potsdamer Platz. A visit to the church was on the agenda. We listened to a reading and the organ, prayed the Lord's Prayer and gave a prayer. We ate Vietnamese food in the Mall of Berlin. On the 2nd floor there is a huge selection of food stores, from boulettes to sushi, so to speak.

In and near Berlin

The afternoon was dedicated to local history. We retraced my old route to school in Neu-Tempelhof. Burgherrenstraße was just like it was back then, only the facades have been freshly painted. Where there used to be allotments, there are now modern apartment buildings. The footpath around the round church still exists, and from the bridge over the "Planschwiese", part of the garden ring, you can already see my school. It used to house the 3rd and 6th elementary school, a practical, technical and science school, and now a secondary school, secondary modern school and grammar school. We then walked back via Parade Street to the subway station of the same name. Buses now run where the streetcar used to go. Well - I always walked to school for 9 years - then as now.

The highlight of our visit to Berlin was a mandolin concert in the evening at the Konzerthaus am Gendarmenmarkt. Il Pomo d'Oro with Avi Avital, Italian baroque. A wonderful concert in a wonderful building, inside and out. And before that the beautiful Christmas market, but we already had that last year. Afterwards we had something Bavarian to eat and drink.

Shortly before midday the next day we headed back to Cologne, the sprint wasn't quite as fast and the connections to Linz were complicated, as Bonn is to be connected to the airport by light rail. But first we took a walk around the Reichstag, fortified by breakfast in the Einstein Café. And as a souvenir and Christmas present, we bought a bear at the hotel, more like a bear with a striped swimsuit and a squeaky duck, with the words "Pack the bathing suit!" on the back says: "Pack your swimming trunks...". Maybe we'll do that when we're in Berlin again, just not before Christmas.

In and near Berlin

Romantic journeys

On the Shannon

Charter boats were very popular in the mid-seventies of the last century. You didn't need a boating license for some areas. So Gunhild and I, then living in Düsseldorf, booked a motor cruiser for a week on the Shannon in beautiful Ireland. As we had to take something with us, we took my car, a VW Beetle. My friend Hans C. had rented a vacation home for himself and his family in Lampeter, in one of the most remote corners of Wales. We came there. There, the air-cooled four-cylinder engine gave up the ghost and a replacement engine had to be found. But that's another story. We finally reached the marina at Killerloe by ferry, train and bus.

Killaloe is a large village in the east of County Clare, Ireland. The village lies on the River Shannon on the western shore of Lough Derg and is connected to the "twin town" of Ballina on the eastern shore of the lake by the Killaloe Bridge.

After the briefing, we set off immediately with the aim of reaching Lough Derg. In Gerrykennedy, there was a small harbor and a store with a pub right behind the refrigerated counter. And in the evening it really got going, I've rarely heard Irish tunes so beautifully. Yes, and the berth was in the harbor.

Garrykennedy is a small town on the opposite side of Lough Derg from Mountshannon. It is a very relaxing and pleasant place on the lough, known for its beautiful views, fishing culture and the famous Larkins thatched house restaurant and music pub.

Now it was on to *Clonmacnoise*, the most famous monastic site in Ireland. The Shannon flows leisurely here, pretty much in the middle of Ireland, with pastureland to the left and right, the very image of the "Emerald Isle". For water lovers, there is a jetty and you walk uphill to the extensive grounds.

Romantic journeys

Clonmacnoise is an old monastery complex near Shannonbridge in County Offaly and one of the most important visitor attractions in Ireland. A walk through the peaceful stone ruins of this famous site will conjure up images of saints and scholars from Ireland's famous golden age of learning.

We reached **Athlone** at the halfway point. This larger town lies roughly in the middle of the entire river trip. You have to go through a lock into the town and there is a strong current at the weir. Athlone is famous for its 12th century castle, which we unfortunately didn't visit. But we did go to a butcher's shop and had a great steak cut for us. They do it with a band saw. It was delicious, I think. We also bought a few LPs from the "Wolfs Tones". They play the old rebel songs from 1916 (Eastern Rising) and the proceeds probably go to the IRA.

The **Easter Rising** was an Irish uprising against British rule that took place in Dublin in April 1916 and accelerated Ireland's secession from the British Empire. The uprising was quickly put down by British forces and was initially considered a failure. Nevertheless, it soon became a powerful symbol and helped to focus the efforts of Irish nationalists to free themselves from centuries of British domination.

On the way back, we kept noticing narrow, tall round towers, mostly on the ruins of monasteries. We had already seen one in the monastery at Clonmacnoise. In Italy it was the campanile, in the Orient the minarets. 1,500 years ago, early Christians founded monastic communities in remote stretches of river where the ruins of monasteries, oratories and round towers can still be seen today and where peace can still be found. They were followed by the Vikings, who sailed upstream into the heart of Ireland.

Romantic journeys

If you drive south past Clonmacnoise, you will reach the Shannon Bridge after 10 km. It is one of the oldest bridges in Ireland and is still in use.

The

Shannonbridge was fortified by the British during the Napoleonic era. Some of the fortifications, including a fort which now houses a restaurant, can still be seen on the west bank of the river.

Now we crossed the large lake **Lough Derg** again into a small branch of the Shannon. Pure wild nature. You just have to discover it. The donkeys send their regards.

The evening before our departure, we had a farewell dinner by the lake. And the next day there was still time to visit **Limerick**.

And another thing: limericks (named after the Irish city of Limerick) are five-line verses that follow a specific rhyme scheme (aabba). The first line usually introduces a person and their geographical origin. The last line usually contains the joking punch line, which is followed by rhyming lines 2 to 4. Here is an example.

Romantic journeys

There once was a dog named Lacelle

Who thought her stuffed animals were real

She wanted to play

With her toys all the day

Until she made them hermeal!

By Mrs. Class

The Treaty Stone is the stone on which the Treaty of Limerick was signed in 1691, sealing the handover of the city to William of Orange

From Limerick we traveled by bus, ferry and train to Swansea in South Wales. There we wanted to pick up the Beetle with the replacement engine from the local VW dealer. But the car wasn't ready yet and the engine hadn't been fitted. I first had to convince the garage that it was my car that we wanted to take to Germany. Our mood wasn't the best either, as we had been standing around at the station half the night. So we had the garage do it and took a room in a guesthouse, slept and later watched a cricket match.

Then we set off slowly because the engine had to be run in first. We took the Dover-Calais ferry, on which the rough sea made me feel terribly sick. Here's a limerick from me in German, Translation follows:

Romantic journeys

Man tut immer so, als ob Reisen

Ein Muss sei, der Stein gar der Weisen

Von fremder Kultur

Bleibt meistens doch nur

Das Wetter, Getränke und Speisen... und anderes.

People always act as if traveling

Is a must, the philosopher's stone even

Of foreign culture

All that remains is usually

The weather, drinks and food... and other things.is a must.

***

Good Friday outing with Eva

I can't remember who came up with the idea of doing the traditional Good Friday outing of the Mainz Fencing Club of 1879 by bike. Ultimately, the idea and its implementation were not the real deal for the person in question. But more on that later.

I bought a folding bike for this purpose. Not really suitable for a longer cycle tour, but easy for someone who probably had little to do with cycling, like my friend Eva. She wasn't keen on top athletic performance either.

So off we went, across the countryside around Mainz, as the pictures show. The folding bike broke down for the first time. Until it was repaired, it was time to relax and watch. Eva with me and Martina next door. Soon we were on our way, Gert got the Martina ready to ride.

The cycling continued. Always through the vineyards or Wingert (to stay in the dialect). The little cyclist is probably Roland's son, if I'm not mistaken. We soon completed the first stage and Eva was still in a good mood. Perhaps because she thought she was already halfway through. But not so with the Mainz fencers.

After a long break, we continued on to the Rhine. Everyone had to go through a narrow underpass. Eva, who is not used to cycling long distances under difficult conditions, had to scrape along, which didn't exactly lift her spirits. And there was a strong headwind on the banks of the Rhine. Eva's mood was completely gone. Only pushing helped.

Somehow the bike tour came to an end and we stopped for a bite to eat, which was always the highlight of the event. Everyone was happy and Eva was especially happy. Well - and when there's such a cuddly little girl sitting next to her. But this obvious happiness didn't last. I had made a different decision. I'm sure she found a nice man, which shouldn't have been difficult given her looks.

Back to the south, sometimes engaged and sometimes married

Back to the south, just like 15 years ago. And again to Lake Garda and again to Venice. And yet completely different in every respect. You are engaged to be married. If no one objects, you can get married after 14 days. This time, the engaged couple were drawn to Lake Garda again. Again by car, at least in a premium class model. Sociologically speaking, they had arrived in the middle class: the fiancée with her own dental practice, the future husband as a graduate engineer with a decent salary and vacation entitlement.

First Hans and now Eleonore had made a stopover in Munich. They visited the Deutsches Museum (Foucault's pendulum, the shipping department, the high-voltage demonstration), walked around the Residenz and through the English Garden and admired Munich in the evening (Marienplatz, Ludwigstraße with the Siegestor). The two pretty ladies stopped for a pint of Munich Hell (presumably in the Augustiner Bierhalle).

Romantic journeys

The couple then moved on. Had heard something about spring in South Tyrol. So to Merano, past Innsbruck, via the Brenner highway. Merano is actually a place for older people, but it's also suitable for younger people, as you can see.

Almost two decades have passed since that trip. Now it's time to sit on the promenade at the Kurhaus again - just like back then. And to stop off again at the typical inns that serve Tyrolean speck platters and wine from Lake Kaltern (light, uncomplicated, convivial, not the kind from Lidl).

Now it was not far to Lago di Garda, the village of the same name on the lake. Just two hours by car. The couple ruled out the possibility of hiking there. Even if they had read the following blog (it didn't exist back then): "Four retired

Romantic journeys

Aussies hiked from Merano to Lake Garda on a self-guided tour. The hotels were great, the organization super and the daily hikes were interesting and challenging with fabulous scenery".

Garda is a romantic place, even though it has just turned spring. It has a very special atmosphere, as you can see from the picture.

The fiancée didn't go out without her Burberry, even while eating ice cream on the lakeside terrace. Two things stand out in the strawberry cup picture: the perfectly pearlescent fingernails and the engagement ring on her right hand. Or was that the converted wedding ring? In any case, it was bought by the fiancé there in Garda, a gold ring with a half-carat diamond, for half a million lire (about 500 DM at the time, the same in euros today). The ring is still worn occasionally today.

From Lake Garda, you can visit the beautiful cities of northern Italy, which is exactly what the two of them did. It doesn't always have to

be Venice. How about Verona or Mantua? Both cities are steeped in history. First there were the Romans, then the Goths, much later the Austrians, and finally the cities belonged to the Kingdom of Italy. In Verona you must visit at least three sights: the Piazza delle Erbe, the center of the medieval city republic Arena of Verona, the best preserved and second largest amphitheater in the world after the Colosseum in Rome and the house of Juliet, "Casa di Giulietta" with the famous balcony where Romeo and Juliet swore eternal love.

Eternal love is one of those things. Unfortunately, it ended with the death of the protagonists.

Mantua is a popular excursion or vacation destination for anyone interested in history or art. The Renaissance has left clearly visible traces here. Unfortunately, many Germans (culture buffs) left out this gem on their way to the beaches on the Adriatic, in the truest sense of the word, Modena and Bologna had to be reached after a long drive and then another 150 km to Rimini.

Have you ever heard of Rigoletto, the legendary court jester in Verdi's opera of the same name? You can visit the Casa del Rigoletto and the character.

A guided tour of the ducal palace is obligatory. The Renaissance really jumps out at you.

"Frenchmen! Oh, how badly you shoot!" Who said that? The folk hero Andreas Hofer when he was shot in Mantua in 1810. The second volley still didn't hit the mark. The final shot to the head did the trick.

The fiancés went out again in Garda in the evening. This time we had 935 km to cover to Cologne, in a quality car (BMW 3 Series, again blue but darker). How to describe the trip, perhaps with less romance but more culture.

***

And now back in Munich, now married. This glass picture above was taken in one of Munich's many restaurants, perhaps in the Nuremberg Bratwurst Glöckle at the cathedral. It probably represents the constellation of the married couple.

Here the couple are probably to meet K. (in the Karl the time, he had doctorate and was councillor, which is years of working as a why he was hanging walking towards Isartor, their mutual friend Gert Valentin Museum). At not yet received his not a medical only awarded after 20 dentist. I still don't know around Munich.

The oneymooners wanted to go to Venice, as befits a wedding trip. They had previously stopped off in Salzburg.

And now finally Bella Venezia.

- no postcard -

The newlyweds had chosen a cozy guesthouse very close to the ghetto, the oldest Jewish quarter in the world. They had to leave their car in the underground parking garage at Piazziale Roma and take a water cab there.

We visited the beautiful palaces on the Canale Grade, as we were there longer than the day tourists. But the not so beautiful Venice.

138

Romantic journeys

It was at its best in the evening. The two of them strolled through the alleyways to Harry's Bar (1323 Calle Vallaresso - 30124 Venezia) near St. Mark's Square on the Canale. It was top-notch and expensive at the time, but it had to be done. After eating at the bar, we had a nice chat with an Italian couple, in English of course. That was really upmarket.

There was also plenty to see during the day. Just take the vaporetto, let yourself be ferried to the Lido, to Morano to see glassblowers or to the dead on Isola di San Michele. Crab, tuna heads, Tyrolean bacon and olives.

Arrivederci Hans and Eleonore or something, that's what Rita Pavone sang back then. Ciao

Venezia. Now it's back to the daily grind for the couple, looking after patients and customers. And, of course, awaiting the arrival of their offspring. What remains is the memory of the Scalzi Bridge and the gondola passing underneath it. The couple recently stood on the bridge again, arriving before a cruise. After 37 years together, with two daughters, a son-in-law and possibly one in the making, and a sweet granddaughter.

"Alla nascita dell'amore gli amanti parlano del futuro; al suo declino parlano del passato. "*

*"At the birth of love lovers speak of the future; at its decline they speak of the past. "

From the writing workshop

Note: The following short stories were written in the writing café of my church community in Cologne under the guidance of journalist Thomas Dahl. They are the weekly homework.

Madness - in bundrein (federal)

Super good or really bad, madness is often used as a superlative, noun or adjective. Like: "I'm insanely happy" or "It's driving me crazy". "This is sheer madness" is ambiguous, the expression can stand for both good and bad things.

During the lock-down, I set about playing a tune on my banjo. I wanted to pick "Cripple Creek" as beautifully as Pete Seeger. But something wasn't right, the banjo, which I had owned for a while, wasn't fretless, the note on the empty side isn't the same in the 12th fret, just an octave higher. You can fix this by moving the bridge over the skin towards or away from the neck. You have to figure it out, the internet makes it possible. I still can't play "Cripple Creek".

In the original, the word "Wahnsinn = Madness" is written over a piano keyboard, which means there must be music involved. Continuing musically and wondering how the now well-tuned banjo would have gone down in the country band I played in a few years ago. It was crazy that the boys, a person almost half a century older than them, had accepted me into their band. They needed a second acoustic guitar and a real western banjo. Age shouldn't matter, should it?

With the "Drunken Ducks" from Erpel*, not from Duckburg, I played the wine queen for the coronation. Jonny Cash up, "Country Roads" down. And there were even three trumpets on the "Burning Ring of Fire". The cajonist sat on his tom-tom box and I had the banjo on my knees, everyone else was on their feet. It was worth it, the fee was later used to buy a drum kit. But I wasn't there anymore. Was it because my banjo sounded bad, because the Epyphon guitar was too cheap or because I wasn't playing professionally at all? Now the banjo is clean as a whistle, even Pete Seeger would have his friends. And my new Blueridge guitar doesn't come from the Blue Mountains.

To conclude, the whole thing was a beautiful madness. I have fond memories of it. I still have the sideburns that Ben Cartwright from the series "Bonanza" would have liked.

Erpel is the German word for a male duck

***

Striking life event (1st level), then event/scene (2nd level), no first-person narrative

„Auf Wiedersehn"

An elderly German couple were waiting for the bus to take them from Anchorage to Seward Small Boat Harbor. The Alaskan cruise started from there. To shorten the wait, the couple decided to go to the Alaska Museum, where the bus departed from.

The museum shows Alaska's history and its inhabitants in dioramas, not only the Inuit in the igloos, but also the local Indian tribes with their respective totem poles, or the Aleut people in their earth dwellings, and last but not least the bush planes. The travel-loving couple from Germany found all this so interesting that they talked about it.

Hearing that German was being spoken, an American woman with a 10-year-old girl approached the couple. The girl understood some German and had been listening. The woman said that her niece went to a German school and that she would like to say something in German. The husband asked the girl: "Do you know what Goodby in German is?". In response, the little girl shyly said: "Auf Wiedersehn".

That was a wonderful vacation experience for the travelers. And another was to follow. As the bus was late, we went to the cafeteria. An All-American girl recommended the freshly baked chocolate cakes with the words: "To day I recommend our Alaskan Chocolate Cake. You will hate it." The German couple accepted the delicious offer. Both girls were right.

***

Sensory impressions (seeing, hearing, smelling, tasting, feeling)

1A view at minus seven degrees azimuth

The view from my bedroom window on the Linzer Höhe looks out towards the Hocheifel, which stands out on the horizon in blue-grey. A light veil of cloud lies low over the low mountain range, higher up the light blue of a late summer sky. The green pastures of the farm that gives the district its name, Roniger Hof, stand out from the swathes that rise along the Rhine ditch and, almost as white as the clouds above, stand out from the treetops in front and the Eifel side.

Fortunately, the building regulations have provided for vistas that make such a view possible in the first place. The sun shines, still low, on the two whitewashed houses. The red bricks of the house on the left form a nice contrast to the small wood behind it. The street is still in the shade, asphalt gray. Only the royal blue of the balcony railings and the blue of the paper garbage cans stand out against the dark green of the plants in the front garden.

There's nothing to hear, it's still early. But the meowing of the pet makes it clear that it has been let out onto the balcony. It's too early for my wife to get up, you can hear her turning around again. The silence doesn't last. You can see experienced women walking past in groups, divided into two groups and separated by time, the "racing mice" and the "mallards", the latter equipped with Nordic walking poles. My wife is one of the gerbils, but they both chatter. And when the going gets tough, the rescue helicopter lands noisily at the nearby hospital.

You can smell the fresh air, perhaps even the morning coffee that is already being prepared. The farmer is not fertilizing his fields in this beautiful weather. Even the cigarette smoke from my tenants on the terrace below me has gone, they're on the early shift. It smells delicious when my neighbor fires up his smoker, or rather his barbecue locomotive, and prepares the barbecue. He only does that on nice weekends and certainly not in the morning.

You can already taste the latte, which you have to enjoy every morning after looking at the view.

You can feel the light, cool wind, which usually blows from the southwest onto the Linzer Höhe. Now it is quite pleasant, later in the year it is stronger and drives the rain, and in winter also the snow, against the view.

If you want to make sense of the view, two songs can help: "Morning has Broken" by Cat Stevens and "See what tomorrow Brings" by Peter, Paul and Mary. Stevens describes the morning, rather after a night well spent, the trio urges us, as the chorus of the song says "Wait just long enough, see what tomorrow brings". The picture tells me: "Wait until the fog clears over the river, the view of the mountains becomes clearer. Expect a friendly day. Embrace it!"

1A view. On days with a wide view, you would discover a number of wind turbines, very small and at the very back of the mountains. You think about the energy transition and consider installing 10 kWh peak photovoltaics aligned to minus 7 degrees azimuth.

***

From the writing workshop

Sensory impressions (see picture)

Meditation in Kölle

Where could the pile of driftwood in the picture be? I looked it up on Google Maps. It is piled up on the Cologne meditation meadow. On the Scheel Sick, just behind the Severin Bridge. The pylon on the left, recognizable on the right behind the bridge, the old town panorama of Kölle: the Chocolate Museum, the tower of the Mediapark, the High Cathedral of Cologne, Groß Sankt Martin, the moored ships and boats as well as the Deutzer and Hohenzollern bridges. In addition, the sky was slightly cloudy. You can see all that.

When I look at this pile of wood, I can't help but think of the flood disaster in the Ahr valley. These could be broken branches that were collected from the Ahr here downstream and put together. You should think about it, but it could be that this pile of wood has been there for a long time. It looks like this.

The wood is stacked so that it can be set alight. Perhaps for a memorial fire after all? My thoughts return to the Great Flood in the Ahr valley.

I leave the question open and remove the pile of wood. I can now see Cologne Cathedral in its entirety, the European Waterway flowing wide and gray in front of me. In my mind's eye, I imagine how I took my test for my inland boating license years ago on these kilometers of the Rhine. Years later, I was tested under sail on the Bevertalsperre reservoir. Which brings us back to the water.

Now I leave my position and walk under the bridge. The full panorama of the old town lies before me. I think of dat Hillige Kölle, the holy and the hypocritical. I have been active in both areas, including overlaps. I held the spiritual office of presbyter and churchwarden, according to the church order of the Protestant Church in the Rhineland, and was a Prussian carnivalist in the school carnival (Stenzelberger Blechfunken) and the congregation also got something out of it. I can still see myself, dressed as St. Peter and complete with halo, parading through the parish in the Veetelszoch. Pastor Ivo Masanek took the opportunity to play "Even St. Peter can see that" several times on the accordion. You could see the unholy fun he was having.

There was no talk of really meditating, just another insight into my time in Cologne. I have to go back past the pile of wood again, so many memories in my head. How do I feel about the pile of driftwood at the meditation site now?

From the writing workshop

***

The subject of guilt

Guilt is a wonderful thing

Guilt is a wonderful thing; if we lacked it, we would be surprised. The following explanations will help you understand this connection. I will give a few examples to support this thesis.

You can do anything with guilt, you can share it, take it upon yourself, reject it, assign it to others, deny it, admit it, forgive it, collect it and whatever else there is. As a noun with a prefix or suffix, guilt can be used as an adjective, as well as an adverb. Just think of the blameless (innocent) child or "blamelessly guilty" in the crime scene. Yes, guilt has made it that far. Isn't that wonderful?

That brings us to the examples. But maybe it's also the wonder. We wonder about many things, good and bad. We rejoice over something with "that's wonderful", we get angry with "you did a wonderful job. It's all your fault." There we go again, the guilt is there. Unfortunately, it has a negative connotation.

It can be changed. I'll give you a positive example: it was your fault when you said I couldn't do it. Now I can! One more thing along these lines: in the Lord's Prayer, we ask God to forgive us our trespasses, just as they forgive those who trespass against us. If you don't do this, you may end up like Matthew chapter 18, verses 23-35. If you read it, you won't find anything miraculous there. Rather the opposite.

Now we waver in our belief in the miraculous in our guilt. We see guilt as a given with all its consequences. Atonement ends in punishment or, at best, the guilt catches up with us again and again. With consequences. Everything comes across as anti-synthetic. Can we overcome this and become synthetic?

What do we make of it when we say guilt is something wonderful but don't believe in miracles? Guilt is a different matter. As already mentioned, it exists in all its linguistic facets. That doesn't make the matter, i.e. a synthesis, any easier.

It could be a matter of layering in order to come to a conclusion. From which angle I can agree. In chemistry, you set yourself a synthesis goal, then proceed to break down the desired product into its structures to see how the organic compound behaves chemically.

Let's leave it to everyone to decide for themselves whether they can agree that guilt is something wonderful. I'll come back to "Schuldlos schuldig", which also exists as a religious song. The refrain goes: "Guiltless guilty and betrayed, you hang between God and the world. You stepped into our war and made peace that lasts forever. Has the miracle been accomplished? Yes, guilt was to blame. And so much for dialectics.

***

Theme: stream of consciousness / Bewusstseinsstrom

En la tienda de ropa - In the clothes shop

I knew it, Ele, women love shortened names, like here for Gabriele Eleonore, twice -ele, once at the back, once at the front and yet all of it, bingo, I want to go to the women's clothing store to look at the beautiful long dresses, just around the corner from the hostel in the pedestrian zone on the Plaza de la Magdalena. Just looking - I don't think so, it's more about waiting patiently away from the changing rooms. Yes - sometimes it's not worth looking there either.

From the writing workshop

She said Hola and Buenas Tardes when she asked the sales assistant if she had the dresses in her size over there. ¿Tiene esta alli en mi taille? She is relying on my profound knowledge of Spanish. The answer "Sí, señora, quere las probar algo?" suggested an understandable sentence. Instead of standing around impassively, I prefer to go outside to the plaza and sit on a bench.

It could have been more comfortable, there are fashion stores that offer the mostly male sufferers a coffee, if it comes up, and depending on the size of their stomach, cookies too. And the occasional pitying look. Now I'm sitting there, it's nice in Andalusia in the afternoon. Why are the locals walking around in winter clothes? They're probably not used to anything.

"And she's staring out of the store - oh, give me a black one." Otto Reuther's couplet about buying blouses comes to mind, I've been sitting here for a while. The poor waiting man has faded, now the shopping is not without meaning. Ah - here she comes, hasn't bought anything. The color wasn't right, nor was the length, and the Spanish woman of the right age has the wrong measurements. Just not Central European.

So that was that, the cup passed. It won't be the last. Will I treat myself to an ice cream to relax? There's an ice cream store diagonally opposite. Bueno Helado con ...

***

Topic: Reviews

Mistakes and difficulties in the social fabric back then, only different today

I've already read a lot of Fontane, especially his major works such as "Effi Briest", "Der Stechlin" and of course "Wanderungen durch die Mark". And now "Irrungen und Wirrungen". I liked the description of the setting of the plot, in this case the up-and-coming Berlin of the Wilhelminian era with its surrounding villages and small towns. What I didn't like, and this is due to the present day, was the rather banal plot in the social structure of the newly formed empire. I am always impressed by Fontane's masterly narrative art with its dialogs that fit in with the times and the social context.

A Mark Brandenburg squire falls in love with Lene, a seamstress. The great love is mutual. The baron feels quite at home in the petty bourgeois milieu.

From the writing workshop

Economic and social constraints force him to give up this love. In the end, each of the two protagonists finds happiness in a marriage "befitting their station", accompanied by the aforementioned trials and tribulations.

Fontane is famous for his description of landscapes, the characters that shape them and the changes that are taking place. This is also the case in this work. I liked the local description near Wilmersdorf at the time. Even better was the language used by the petty bourgeoisie and the lower nobility. Here the light Berlin dialect, not the Berlin dialect of the urban proletariat, there the stilted language of the nobility with all kinds of foreign words, mainly in the style of Prussian guard officers. Both social classes are well aware that the old is going, the new is coming, it can be seen everywhere.

It is not my place to criticize a famous poet. Only - the dialogues and thoughts of the characters seem a little long-winded to me, sometimes even boring, if they do not contribute to their characterization. You also have to imagine some actions, which are among the most normal things. Describing these was considered immoral at the time.

What if a novel of this kind were to be rewritten today? What would the protagonists be, what exactly would the plot be like? Perhaps something copied from the British aristocracy or a bit of a Cinderella story with a bad ending. I mean, not much different, just more modern.

That said, it is a work by a great storyteller that is well worth reading. Not necessarily suitable as a bestseller, more suitable for the advanced German course when it comes to literary realism or simply relaxing reading of an elevated kind.

Apart from its literary significance, the book provides a unique insight into Berlin's past, the imperial era of the Gründerzeit, when Berlin was not yet a major city. Theodor Fontane lived with his family in the middle of it all, in Kreuzberg, Potsdamer Strasse 134 c. Irrungen und Wirrungen, Theodor Fontane, 208 pages, ISBN 978-3-458-35221-1, € 5.00, paperback, Insel Verlag, published in 2008

Betroffen von einem Regentropfen

Ein Regentroffen fällt ins Meer,
es schmeckt salzig.

Er trifft auf unzählige Lebewesen,
so groß wie er.

Weiter entdeckt er silberne Fische in
Schwärmen,

große Fische werfen ihre Schatten
darauf.

Der Regentropfen lässt sich fallen,
in die Tiefe.

Jetzt hört er die Laute der
Meeressäuger und

immer wieder leuchtet ein
Tiefseewesen.

Von oben kommt ein Geräusch.

Neugierig steigt er hoch, das
Geräusch wird lauter und

nimmt ihm mit, im Strudel der
Propeller.

Noch hört er Stimmen und Musik,
es riecht nach verbranntem Treibstoff
und frischer Farbe, er fühlt sich leicht,

dann löst er sich im Dunst des
Fahrwassers auf.

Im Dunst geht es hoch in den blauen
Himmel,

die Töpfchen wachsen, eine Wolke
entsteht.

Aus ihr fällt ein neuer Regentropfen,
vielleicht ins Meer?

Affected by a raindrop

A raindrop falls into the sea,
it tastes salty.

He encounters countless
creatures as big as himself.

Further on he discovers silver
fish in shoals,

large fish cast their shadows on
it.

The raindrop drops into the
depths.

Now he hears the sounds of
marine mammals and

again and again a deep-sea
creature shines.

A sound comes from above.

Curious, he climbs up, the sound
gets louder and

takes him with it, in the whirl of
the propellers.

He can still hear voices and
music,

The smell of burnt fuel and fresh
paint, he feels light,

then it dissolves into the haze of
the fairway.

In the haze, it goes up into the
blue sky,

the pots grow, a cloud forms.

A new raindrop falls from it,
perhaps into the sea?

Poems

Beyond Eighty

Beyond Eighty hört sich besser an als **Über Achtzig**,

Achtzig Plus wäre auch nicht schlecht.

Eighty Plus ist auch scharmant,

kling aber nach **After Eight**

Mit Achtzig liegt man in der Gewinnzone,

sagt die Deutsche Rentenversicherung.

Beyond the Break-even Point.

Wenn die Gesundheit stimmt, hat man ehedem gewonnen.

Before Eighty war, lange Jahre voller Erinnerungen,

die einem bleiben. Wird sich noch einiges erfüllen?

Sicherlich gibt es Schmerzhaftes zu erleben,

Freunde, Verwandte, gar Angehörige werden gehen,

für immer. **Beyond!**

Vom Gewohntem wird man sich verabschieden - müssen,

nach und nach.

Mit **Beyond Eighty** kann man was anfangen.

Es steht für Weiteres, für Weitermachen, auch für Beibehalten.

Für Freude an der Kultur, ebenso am Sport, mit und ohne Teilhabe.

Hoffnung auf Erfolgsgeschichten der Kinder,

auf das Fortkommen der Enkelkinder.

All das mitzuerleben „**it´s not Beyond me**", geht mir nicht über den Horizont.

Beyond Eighty

Beyond Eighty sounds better than over eighty,

Eighty Plus wouldn't be bad either.

Eighty Plus is also charming,

but sounds like After Eight

Eighty puts you in the profit zone,

says the German Pension Insurance.

Beyond the break-even point.

If you're in good health, you've already won.

Before Eighty was, long years full of memories,

that stay with you. Will some things still come true?

There will certainly be painful experiences,

Friends, relatives, even loved ones will leave,

forever. Beyond!

We will have to say goodbye to the familiar - bit by bit,

little by little.

You can do something with *Beyond Eighty*.

It stands for going further, for moving on, for keeping on.

For enjoyment of culture and sport, with and without participation.

Hope for children's success stories,

for the progress of grandchildren.

Experiencing all this *"it's not Beyond me"* is not beyond me.

Poems

Gedicht vom Mithalten

Will ich, kann ich, muss ich – mithalten?
Für wen, mit wem und warum?
Mithalten für wen, zunächst für mich,
etwa für die Familie, Freunde, gar Fremde?
Mithalten mit wem, mit all den andern
In meinem Alter, etwa mit den Jungen?
Und warum? Keine Antwort oder doch eine.

Muss ich auch Mitmachen?
Ja, sonst kann ich nicht mithalten
Aber wie, wo, für was?
Ein bisschen mitmachen oder voll drauf,
innerlich, äußerlich, nur so
Für was lohnt es sich, das Muss
Gewinn oder Verdruss.

Muss ich – mitschwimmen, mitlaufen, mitgehen, mitreden?
Muss ich mich also bewegen,
mit den anderen, auf gleiche Höhe,
von unten nach oben oder umgekehrt,
körperlich, geistig, so tun als ob?
Ich sinne nach, über die Vorsilbe „mit"
Geht's denn nicht ohne?

Mithalten, doch lieber loslassen
Mitmachen, doch lieber machen lassen
Mitschwimmen, doch lieber allein die Bahn ziehen
Mitgehen, doch lieber stehen bleiben
Mitlaufen, doch lieber zurückbleiben
Mitreden, doch lieber sich überredenlassen
Ich schwanke, muss ich, muss ich nicht – hier und dort,
außer wenn ich will und kann.

Poems

Ich muss nicht, aber könnte, wenn ich wollte.
Wenn ich muss, dann kann ich vielleicht nicht.
Und wollen tue ich es bestimmt nicht
Alle müssen, zuletzt, dann können wir nicht anders,
ob wir wollen oder nicht.
Auch da halten wir mit, mit dem Leben mithalten
müssen wir dann nicht. Auf zum Großen Manitou.

Poem about keeping up

Do I want to, can I, must I - keep up?
For whom, with whom and why?
Keeping up for whom, first of all for me,
for family, friends, even strangers?
Keeping up with whom, with all the others
At my age, for example with the boys?
And why? No answer, or one.

Do I also have to take part?
Yes, otherwise I can't keep up
But how, where, for what?
Join in a little or go all out,
inwardly, outwardly, just like that
For what is it worthwhile, the must
Profit or annoyance.

Do I have to - swim along, run along, walk along, talk along?
So I have to move,
with the others, on the same level,
from the bottom to the top or vice versa,
physically, mentally, pretending?
I think about the prefix "with"
Can't we do without it?

Keep up, but rather let go
Join in, but rather let it happen
Swim along, but rather pull the course alone
Walk along, but rather stand still

Poems

Run along, but rather stay behind
Have a say, but prefer to be persuaded
I waver, I have to, I don't have to - here and there, unless I want to and can.

I don't have to, but I could if I wanted to.
If I have to, then maybe I can't.
And I certainly don't want to
We all have to, in the end, we can't help it,
whether we want to or not.
We keep up with that too, keep up with life
we don't have to. On to the Great Manitou.

Hörnchennudel-Gedicht

Ich war ein Glückspilz, gewesen

War davon genesen, vom Pilz

War ruhig und angepasst, fast

Zum Glück nicht ganz erblasst

Bin gern auf dieser Welt, doch ich

Traue ihr nicht so recht, nicht

Bin auf dem Weg der Besserung

Zeig noch keine Verbitterung

Werde sein ein Mensch, tolerant

Ich werde nicht sein dominant

Werde Musik immer lieben

weiter von Klängen getrieben

Croissant noodle poem

I was a lucky man, had been

Had recovered from it, from the mushroom

Was calm and adapted, almost

Fortunately not quite pale

I like being in this world, but I

Don't really trust it, not

On the road to recovery

Show no bitterness yet

Be a human being, tolerant

I will not be dominant

Will always love music

Continue to be driven by sound

Created on 09.03.23, 11:38 am, there is chicken soup with croissant noodles in it.

Short Stories

A misleading encounter

"Good evening," says the morning sky to the evening sky. "Good morning," he replies and continues: "Well, I find it strange that we're meeting, but it's a way for me to get to know you."

"Oh yes, I wanted to, but somehow it didn't work out," replies the morning sky, "tell me, how are you?" The evening sky contorts its face, dark clouds appear on it and says anxiously: "Oh, I think a thunderstorm is approaching. Happens to me more often, but I can do otherwise."

The evening sky now tells of his appearance in Aqaba: "The people have just returned from their trip from the rock city of Preta on the cruise ship, they are on the upper deck and admire me as I stage myself over the Sinai desert." "I could still be happy about it today if some of the passengers hadn't sung the Capri Fishermen, you know the hit song by Rudi Schurike - 'When the red sun sinks into the sea at Capri'. I'm telling you, it can make you lose your appetite."

"Yes, that's how it goes," agrees the morning sky, "sometimes it makes you cry, people call it rain and think they're having a bad day." "But I can tell you better things." "When I think of Bella Italia, and I'll leave out Capri," the morning sky continues, "my performance in Gatteo al Mare comes to mind. The people there, mainly older German early risers, sit at the mouth of the Rubicon and watch as I flaunt myself across the Adriatic, the dew sparkling in the fishermen's nets. After I leave, the café bars around me are already serving cappuccino, cornetti and cantuccini. From somewhere I can still hear 'Mornig has broken', the song by Cat Stephens."

"You're giving people a lot of friends," remarked the evening sky, "I also like to watch people having a good time in the garden pubs." "But on a different note, when are you going on vacation?"

The morning sky thinks for a moment and then says: "If I want to do that, I have to cross the Arctic Circle in summer. I only have to make one effort, then I'll have my peace and quiet for a few weeks. The people there call it the White Nights."

"Yes," says the evening sky, "it's the other way around for me. I also have to cross the Arctic Circle, but the people there always grumble something like 'It's always so dark'. You can't please them either."

"By the way, do you know," the morning sky starts again, "that we're sort of brothers. Just think about it." The evening sky thinks and answers: "Could it be that our father is the day and our mother is the night? Mother is the one who puts me to bed."

"Yes," confirms the morning sky, "and father throws me out of bed. But I wonder why we haven't met before, since we are a family?"

"I'd like to know that too," says the evening sky, "it was nice to meet you." "I think so too," says the morning sky in agreement, "well, goodbye then, see you again."

***

The dream of a sharp cut

Next to me, I hear a gentle inhalation and exhalation, quiet and regular. Not like at the doctor's - "Now take a deep breath in and out." My wife has fallen asleep, I haven't yet. Because I had read one of Edgar Allan Poe's eerie stories to help me fall asleep. To take my mind off it, I think about the beautiful winter walk I took this morning in our beautification area. The idyll by the flowing stream finally puts me to sleep.

A man of indeterminate age with dark but equally indeterminate clothing enters the cutlery store. The name of the store is "Schneidwaren Köpfer - sale and repair of all types of cutlery". The indeterminate man is carrying a flat but heavy parcel wrapped in waterproof packing paper. The salesman, a man in his fifties, a typical family man, apparently Mr. Köpfer himself, greets the customer. The following dialog develops:

"I have a cutting tool here that needs sharpening," says the nondescript

man, unwrapping a large steel blade with a slanted edge, "You have a sharpening shop here, don't you?" "Yes, we do. But it's unusual work," the family man leans over the customer's goods, "Ah, Sheffield Steel, good quality. What are the 3 holes on the straight side for?"

"Screws go through there so that the cutting blade can be attached to the head," comes the answer from the vague man, "That's the head that is inserted

157

into the grooves. And occasionally there is a second one, which we insert into the bezel. But this one doesn't stay there for long." The man smiles subtly.

Slightly confused, the salesman looks at the customer, who is looking a little scary. He feels compelled to explain: "The Board of Trustees thinks we should put the furniture we found in a side of the criminal court back in its old place. It's a room adjoining the building, tiled in white with a tiled floor. Everything is easy to clean. The furnishings are to be placed there and can be used. As a museum piece of criminal history and for possible use. After all, the board of trustees believes that life depictions bring life, even if only briefly, to the museum."

"You were talking about use, I think you mean execution, there's no penalty for that in Germany," the father of the family has now realized what it's all about. "Yes, there is," the vague man replied. "Tomorrow you will find the following in the Federal Law Gazette: Anyone who interferes with road traffic by sticking to a carriageway and thus disrupts public order does so for the last time."

"Is that safe?" asks the store owner. "Dead sure!" the vague man tells him. The owner looks depressed, as he knows that his son wants to set off tomorrow for the taping. He is disturbed by the customer's question as to when he can have the sharpened drop knife back. The answer is in 3 days.

The vague man nods and says: "Oh, maybe you can help. I'd like to have the catcher basket repaired, it's bumped, six kilos per head is quite a lot. But it's already been cleaned. And a plastic catcher is out of the question because of the reverence, everything has to be original."

"I can help you with that. Go around the corner two streets away, there's a guy who does repairs like that."

"Maybe he can also help me refurbish the device. The barrel grooves are dirty from the soft soap and it's still sticky at the bottom."

"I don't know, the man has experience, he might be willing to do it."

"And if I'm lucky, he has connections with a mortician and is familiar with the logistics there. I'm only responsible for the operational process. Yes, an instrument like this is a lot of work, but it's precise. It used to be all manual work, but where can you find skilled workers for that nowadays, given the shortage?"

The "Have a nice day" did not go down well with Mr. Köpfer. But business is business, after all, he didn't want to be part of the last generation. Not him and certainly not his son. Or did he just dream the encounter?

"You're snoring like a bear in hibernation, but you're snorting, did you have a bad dream?" my wife wakes me up. "How do you know how bears snore in winter?" I reply, not exactly quick-witted. But I don't wait for an answer and admit to having had a strange dream. Did what I dreamed really happen, so close to reality, or do doubts arise? The dream was so vivid and then the plausible conversation.

I didn't want to come to my wife in the morning with what Edgar Allan Poe meant in his poem: whether life is just an illusion, with all our doubts and uncertainty about the nature of reality. Your answer to this would only be: Don't worry about it. Out of the dream - make us a cappuccino instead.

What is Poe meaning of the poem?

The poem expresses doubt and uncertainty about the nature of reality, questioning whether life itself is just an illusion—"a dream within a dream."

***

Spanish children's lie

It all fits together: The dentist's grandma, the grandpa with his Spanish, the grandchild who is about to lose his milk teeth and a story that isn't true. The story of the little mouse Pérez, el ratoncito Pérez.

There was once an oyster that was very sad Habia una vez una ostra, que estaba muy triste.

"What happened to you?" asked her friend Octopus, who lived at the bottom of the sea. ¿Que te pasa? Le preguntó su amigo el pulpo, que vivia el fondo del mar.

"I lost my pearl," replied the oyster He perdido mi perla - espondió la ostra.

"What was the pearl like?" asked the octopus. ¿Cómo era la perla? Preguntó el pulpo.

"White, hard, small and shiny," replied the oyster. Blanca, duro, pequeña y brillante-contestó la ostra.

The octopus promised to help her and left. He found a turtle on the beach and explained the oyster's problem. The turtle promised to help her and left. She found a little mouse walking around the stall. The mouse's name was Pérez.

La ostra ha perdido su perla. Tenemos que buscar algo blanca, duro, pequeña y brillante- dijo la tortuga al ratón. "The oyster has lost its pearl. We have to look for something white, hard, small and shiny," said the tortoise to the mouse.

The little mouse began to search for an object with these characteristics. First he found a button, which was white, shiny and small, but not hard. Then he found a stone, which was white, small and hard, but not shiny. Finally, he found a coin, which was white, hard and shiny, but not small.

The mouse returned home, sad and disappointed. The mouse's home is in a child's room under the wardrobe. On the bedside table he found a milk tooth, which he examined: it was white, small, hard and shiny.

She then took the tooth and exchanged it for the silver coin. Later she ran to the beach and gave the tooth to the turtle, the turtle to the octopus and the octopus to the oyster, which was very pleased because the tooth was very similar to the lost pearl. She picked it up and nobody noticed the difference.

Therefore, and since then, whenever a child loses a milk tooth and puts it under the pillow, at night the little mouse comes looking for it, finds it and exchanges it for a coin. Por so, desde entonces, cuando un niño pierde un diente de leche, lo pone de la almohada y por la noche el ratoncito Pérez viene a buscarlo y lo cambia por dinero.

Now the dentist's grandma has got rid of her story, the grandpa has written something in Spanish, the grandchild knows what's coming and it's all true, isn't it?

***

Closing words

I have written down my memories here and told you how my life began in Berlin, which at that time was still the Prussian capital and imperial capital. The whole city of Berlin became a divided city, there was a West Berlin and an East Berlin. I described what life was like in West Berlin in ten-year increments. After my studies, I moved to the west of the Federal Republic of Germany, followed by years of hard work. Then I had everything: a family and a house and so on. I ended up in middle-class society. My wife and I have been retired from working life for some time and have raised our daughters in the meantime. They have found their partners and also started a family. So we are grandparents.

But the memories that we have collected over a long life remain, and there is still a lot to come before our end. Until then, we will see our granddaughters grow up, go to school, make friends and perhaps go to university one day. And their parents will remember us.